The Saturday Girl

Chapter one

The weather had been really kind to us over the Easter holidays; the bright warm sunshine tempting people out of their Winter hibernation like plants springing out of the dark earth to seek the light. The magnificent vistas and pure air of the Lake District National Park attracted visitors like a magnet as they hurried to escape the urban landscapes of everyday life. This meant an upsurge in custom for the area's shops and eating establishments and we were no exception; the Toasted Bun Tea Room in the village of Underwood was often bursting at the seams with hungry tourists.

I'm far from complaining but by the time the holiday period was over my trusty sidekick, Olive, and I were worn out and ready for a break ourselves. Unfortunately, with a busy Summer season on the horizon this wasn't going to happen. The best I could do for Olive was to include a nice fat bonus in her pay packet but what was the point of having money if you were too tired to enjoy it.

Of course we'd been through busy seasons before without any trouble but I found that this year I was dreading what was to come.It was at this point that I had to face facts; neither of us was getting any younger and we needed some help. I was unsure how Olive would react to the idea of another member of staff; it had been just the two of us for so long and she didn't always accept change easily. I would have to pick my moment to broach the subject. It came one morning whilst we were having a well earned tea break between the breakfast and lunchtime rushes.

"I've been thinking," I said.

"Mm" said Olive, engrossed in the latest edition of her favourite magazine.

"I've been thinking that we could do with some help in the busy periods."

Olive's head shot up - I'd captured her attention. Her expression was something between interested and wary.

"Had you someone in mind?" she asked.

"No, I thought I might put an advert in the window."

A frown appeared between her brows.

"I know you have to be careful how you word things these days" she said, " but we need someone...well...young."

"I agree with you," I said, "I was hoping to attract a student who could do weekends during term time and more hours during the holidays."

"Perfect," she said, pushing her magazine to one side, "I'll bring you some card and a pen; you can do it right now."

I had to chuckle at her eagerness but it brought home to me that although she would never complain, she must be struggling with the workload.

I was hoping for a quick response to the advert but I was surprised when, whilst I was filling the dishwasher with the lunchtime pots, Olive popped her head round the kitchen door to tell me there was someone enquiring about the job. I could tell by her expression that she wasn't impressed with the applicant.

"Who is it?" I whispered.

"Come and see for yourself."

Apprehensively I walked into the shop to see one of our regular customers, Mrs Morrison, standing by the counter. My heart fell to my boots; Mrs Morrison was a lovely lady but she must have been in her seventies. She greeted me with a wide smile.

"Hello Harriet, I've just seen the card in the window advertising for help. Is the job still vacant?"

I invited her to sit with me at one of the empty tables. "Yes it is" I said and then hesitated about how to continue without offending.

"Oh that's good," she said eagerly.

"I have to stress," I said "that the work can be very tiring at busy times."

"I should think it is but that won't be a problem."

I was getting worried. "It might involve some heavy lifting."

"That's fine, she's a strong girl."

"And the hours - did you say she?"

"Yes my granddaughter, Sophie."

She must have seen the relief on my face and started to laugh. "Oh Harriet, you didn't think I was asking for myself?"

"I'm afraid I have to admit I did and I was rather worried."

She shook her head. "My working days are well and truly behind me but my sixteen year old granddaughter is staying with me at the moment and she could do with the money."

I immediately thought of a problem. "How long will she be staying with you because I was hoping for someone long term."

She sighed. "She could be with me for some time; she's had a big fall out with her mother. They clash quite a lot; you know how it is."

I thought about the arguments I'd had with my own daughter before she went to university;they might have got heated at times but they'd never been bad enough for her to leave home.

"But what if they make up and she goes back?"

"That's still not a problem; she only lives in the next village and she has a bike."

I was satisfied with that and said "Why don't you ask her to pop in and see me after school? I can have a chat with her about it."

"Thank you so much" said Mrs Morrison as she stood to leave, "I'd really appreciate it." then she seemed to hesitate.

"I just have to ask you not to be put off by her appearance; she's a little unconventional but she's a good girl."

As I watched her turn and wave as she closed the door behind her a niggle of unease ran through me. What did she mean by not being put off by her appearance?

Of course I would now have to give inform Olive of what had been said in the conversation but I should have guessed there'd be no need; she had been eavesdropping from the kitchen doorway.

"That sounds ominous; I wonder what she looks like."

"I don't know but if she's not suitable I don't have to hire her."

I spent the rest of the afternoon in a state of apprehension waiting for the monster from the black lagoon to come through the door and let my imagination run wild to the extent that when, finally, around four thirty when the ogre manifested itself I was pleasantly surprised and not a little relieved.

The first thing I noticed about the girl, who came marching in through the door, was her smile; a lovely warm smile that spread across her face and which you couldn't help but return. It was only afterwards that you noticed the shock of bright pink hair standing up in spikes all over her scalp, the multiple piercings up the length of her ears, in her eyebrow and the sparkling stud nestled at the side of her nose.

"Mrs Jones?" she asked as she approached the counter.

"Yes" I said "and you must be Sophie."

She held out her hand for me to shake. "That's me; I believe my nan spoke to you about the job. Is it still vacant?"

"It is" I said and like I'd done with her nan I invited her to sit with me at one of the tables. Olive had gone home and we had no other customers so I put the closed sign on the door before I sat down

I went through the essentials such as the hourly rate, working hours and so on and she was quite happy with these. The prospect of more hours during holiday periods was also eagerly accepted so we could move on to a more relaxed chat.

"I suppose you must be taking yourb GCSE's at the moment, are you planning to go on and do your 'A' levels?" I asked.

Sophie pulled a face. "Yes but I'm not sure what subjects to choose; I suppose it depends on my GCSE grades."

"What would you really like to do?"

"D'you know Mrs Jones I haven't the foggiest; I'm hoping for some inspiration in my results."

I liked the girl's honesty; there was no pretention about her, what you saw was what you got and I liked that so I made my decision.

"Would you like to start on Saturday?"

Her smile was eager. "Oh yes please."

We shook hands on it. "See you Saturday then" I said.

She almost skipped out of the door and I had a good feeling about her but I suspected Olive would have something to say when she saw her and I allowed myself a naughty giggle at the thought of it.

The next morning when Olive arrived for work she was eager for news and I was pleased to tell her that our new member of staff would be starting on Saturday.

"She was suitable then?"

"Yes her name's Sophie and she's a lovely girl; she'll be doing weekends, ten 'til four."

I knew what Olive's next question would be.

"What was she like?"

"I told you, she's a lovely girl."

"Harriet Jones you know what I mean. What did she *look* like? Didn't Mrs Morrison say not to be put off by her appearance?"

I thought about it for a moment. "Let's say she's an individual."

"You're hiding something" said Olive with a look that made me think she was going to shine a light in my eyes and give me the third degree. "Was she wearing odd clothes or something?"

I tried to keep my face straight. "No, she was wearing her school uniform actually."

"What about her hair?"

"Yes she definitely had hair."

I was saved from further interrogation by a loud knock on the back gate.

"That'll be the milkman" I said, "I'd better go and pay him."

Luckily by the time I got back the tea room was filling up and Olive was busy serving customers. I hoped she'd drop the subject because I didn't want to spoil the 'surprise'. I should have known better because as soon as there was a lull in custom she cornered me in the kitchen.

"Right Harriet Jones, come clean; there's something you're not telling me."

"Alright" I said, holding up my hands in submission, "I give in."

I gave her a full description but didn't get the reaction I'd expected.

"Is that all? I think I can cope with that" she said; "My sister's granddaughter went through a similar phase and she's a lovely girl. People should never be put off by appearances."

I looked at Olive through different eyes and remembered why I liked her so much.

Chapter two

Sophie was early on her first day which I admired because it showed that she was either eager or wanting to make a good impression.

"Good morning Mrs Jones" she said as she almost danced through the front door. "I hope I'm not too early."

"Not at all. Good morning to you and you can call me Harriet."

At the sound of our voices Olive came out of the kitchen and stood beside me. "And I'm Olive, come with me and we'll sort you out with an apron."

Sophie frowned and looked down at what she was wearing. "Are these clothes not suitable?"

I looked at the baggy top, short skirt, stripey tights and bright red Doc Martens and said "They're absolutely fine but you don't want to spill something down them and get them spoiled."

Her expression brightened. "Oh I see what you mean, well let's see what you've got."

Olive led her into the kitchen and offered her a plain white full apron but Sophie was eying up the selection hanging on the peg. "Can I wear that one?"

She was pointing to one that we kept as a spare. A customer had bought Olive and I one each last Christmas and it sported a bold paisley pattern containing all the colours of the spectrum."

"If you like" said Olive, taking it down for her.

She tried it on and gave us a twirl. "Ta da" she exclaimed with a beaming smile which made both Olive and I laugh; I realised that life was never going to be dull when Sophie was around and I looked forward to it.

I started her off with simple tasks such as clearing tables and washing the pots. We had a dishwasher and Olive showed her how it worked.

"We tend to only use it at busy times" she said; "when there's only a few we tend to do them in the sink because it's quicker and less hassle but don't worry about your nails, we've got rubber gloves."

Sophie picked up a pair in bright yellow and tried them on ; she pretended to admire them.

"Not in this season's colour" she said in a 'posh' voice "but one could get used to them."

Olive and I looked at each other and shared a secret smile.

Sophie proved her worth at lunchtime when we were really busy. In between carrying out the jobs I'd given her she also waited on tables while Olive and I took orders and prepared food. She seemed to know instinctively what was needed and required little instruction. If she carries on like this, I thought, she's going to be a real asset.

Around three o' clock Mrs Morrison dropped in, supposedly for a cup of tea but I suspected it was really to see how Sophie was getting on. She sat at one of the tables a fair distance from the counter and waited for me to go over and take her order.

"How's she doing?" she asked in a whisper.

"She's doing wonderfully" I said; "she's in the kitchen at the moment, emptying the dishwasher. Shall I tell her you're here."

"No, I don't want to interrupt her work."

At that moment Sophie came out of the kitchen with a trayful of clean mugs for the coffee machine. She spotted us straight away.

"Hiya Nan have you come to check up on me?"

"No, I was just…"

"I know what you were just doing" said Sopie and she came over and gave her nan a big

hug.

"I've told her you're doing great" I said, "now why don't you take your nan's order, get yourself a drink and sit down with her and have a break."

"Thanks Harriet, if you're sure." said Sophie.

I watched them from the counter; they were in animated conversation when the door opened and a young man walked in. They both looked up and Mrs Morrison's manner changed.

"What's he doing here?" she demanded.

Sophie seemed as surprised as her nan. "I don't know."

The young man made a beeline for their table. "Hi Mrs Morrison, Sophie, I thought I'd pick you up after work."

"She's not finished yet" snapped Mrs Morrison and if looks could kill as they say…

"It's okay Nan, I'll deal with it."

The young man frowned and Sophie said "I told you I don't finish until four o' clock and then I'm going straight home to get changed."

"I can wait" he said, starting to pull back a chair to sit down but Sophie stopped him.

"Go home Brad and I'll see you later."

He shrugged his shoulders. "Okay if that's what you want. I'll see you later then."

When he reached the door he turned and said "By the way, nice pinny."

Mrs Morrison opened her mouth to speak but Sophie cut her short. "Not here Nan, *please*"

"Alright but we'll talk about it when you get home."

With those words she stood up and left, leaving her cup of tea untouched.

I didn't say anything because I could see that Sophie was upset and as there'd been no trouble it was really none of my business.

With her chin nearly touching her chest Sophie cleared the table they'd been using and took the pots to the kitchen. Olive had already left for the day so I left her alone until she was ready. When she came back into the shop her mascara was smudged and her eyes were still full of tears.

"I'm sorry about what happened before" she said.

"It's okay" I said, "it sorted itself out. Was that your boyfriend?"

"Yes but I'm going to finish with him later."

"I take it your Nan doesn't like him"

"She has good reason."

She didn't elaborate so I changed the subject. "Anyway, how did you like your first day?"

I was pleased to see the smile return to her face. "I've loved it; thanks for giving me this chance Harriet."

"You're welcome; you've been a big help to us today and once you've settled in we won't know how we managed without you.

Her smile broadened and lit up her eyes drying away the last remnants of tears. I looked at the clock.

"It's nearly four so why don't you get off home and take what's left of that lemon meringue pie; I know it's one of your Nan's favourites."

She did as she was told and waved to me through the door as she closed it behind her.

I'd meant what I said to her but a reservation nagged in my brain and I hoped I hadn't taken on trouble.

Chapter three

It was Sophie,herself, who brought the subject up the next day but not straight away. She'd hardly managed to swap her coat for her apron before the tearoom started to get busy. It was a beautiful late Spring morning; one of those I call a good to be alive day when the early morning dew evaporates as the sun warms up in a cloudless blue sky. Such a morning brings the ramblers out early and by mid-morning they're ready for sustenance to fuel them until lunch.

As on the previous day Sophie worked diligently without needing any instruction, leaving Olive and I free to take orders and prepare food. There was no time for conversation, except with the customers, for some time so it was much later in the day that she managed to speak to me alone. Olive was managing to cope on her own in the tearoom while I whipped up a fresh batch of scones for the following day and Sophie was handwashing a few straggling pots in the sink.

"My nan said thanks for the lemon meringue pie" she said, "we had it after tea and she really enjoyed it."

I smiled at her. "That's lovely; it's nice to get an unexpected treat sometimes."

"And I'm sorry about the other business, you know, with Brad. I promise it won't happen again."

"Let's forget about it" I said, stooping to put the baking tray in the oven. "Did you manage to sort things out with him."

"I hope so; I don't like upsetting Nan, she's been so good to me."

I stood up and stretched my back before asking "How long have you been living with her?"

"A couple of months. I had a big row with my mum - partly over Brad but there was lots of other stuff as well." She broke into a wide grin. "She wasn't happy with what she called my fashion sense."

I smiled. "Well my motto is if it suits the wearer…"

"Precisely" she said.

"What about your dad, what did he think."

"He's more understanding." She grinned again. "Nan said he was also one of a kind when he was my age."

"I see" I said, matching her grin. "What changed him?"

She sighed and pulled a wry face. "He met Mum."

We both laughed out loud drawing Olive in from the shop.

"What's going on?" she asked. "What am I missing?"

Sophie told her what she'd said and with a straight face Olive replied "I know what you mean, Norman did the same to me."

We all laughed and Sophie said "Oh Olive I can just imagine you with with a nose ring and bright pink hair."

"Cheeky!" said Olive and laughed even louder.

Trade was a little slower the following day which was typical of the time of year when only the odd lucky few were able to extend their weekend by one more day. This was when our local custom was really important and I made sure I looked after my regulars.

Mrs Morrison wasn't one of our *most* regulars but came in quite often so it wasn't a surprise when she came in that morning. She sat at a table well away from the counter and smiled up at me when I went over to take her order.

"First of all Harriet, thank you for the pie you sent home with Sophie."

"She's already passed on your thanks" I said "and I told her you were most welcome."

She hesitated before going on. "I also want to apologise for leaving so rudely the other day."

"Don't worry about it; I could see you were upset."

"That lad has caused so much trouble for Sophie; he was one of the reasons she left home."

"Yes she told me about that."

"It was why I was so pleased you'd given her the job; I thought it would keep her out of his way and I'd hate him to spoil it for her."

I sat down next to her, put my order pad down on the table and took her hand in mine."

"Sophie is a good worker and has settled in really well. She gets on well with both Olive and myself and is brilliant with the customers. We're not going to let him spoil it Mrs Morrison."

She smiled and covered my hand with the one I wasn't holding. "Please call me Irene."

"Well then Irene, what can I get you to drink?"

She ordered a pot of tea and a toasted tea cake. I would have sat with her for a while but we were starting to get busy so I served her and left her to enjoy her breakfast.

When the rush was over and Irene had left Olive came over to me.

"I saw you talking to Mrs Morrison earlier, was she wanting a progress report on Sophie?"

"Sort of" I said being a little non-committal, "I suppose it's only natural for her to be concerned."

"I suppose so" said Olive with a shrug of her shoulders but she didn't probe any further. I was glad because Olive hadn't been present when the incident occurred; I could tell she'd taken to Sophie and I didn't want to spoil that. Anyway, I decided, Sophie must have settled things with Brad because he didn't come in again.

One visitor we did have was our local policeman, P.C. Richards.

"Hello Pete" I said "We've missed you. You've not been in for your elevenses for a while."

"I've been on nights," he explained. "There's been a spate of burglaries in this area recently and the boss wanted extra manpower."

"Have they caught the culprits then?"

"Not yet but things seemed to have quietened down for the moment."

"Perhaps they've moved on."

"That's possible but I'd take extra care with locking up both here and at home." He looked over my shoulder. "That goes for you as well Olive."

Gradually Sophie settled in more and more until I began to wonder how we'd ever managed without her. Both Olive and I took her to our hearts and she became a full member of our little working family. One Saturday morning, therefore, both Olive and I noticed something different about her. She was as warm and friendly as ever but every now and then she stopped and seemed to drift off into a world of her own. In the end I was forced to ask "Sophie are you okay? You don't seem yourself today."

She looked at me as though waking from a dream and then smiled.

"I think I'm in love" she said.

"Oh I see." I tried not to laugh at her blissful expression and deep wistful sigh.

"His name's Ryan and I met him last night." She blushed under her flawless mask of foundation and lowered her eyes. I hoped she'd not done something she'd regret.

"I went to a gig in the community centre in Dunsfield with my mate Nina from school" she carried on "and he was there with his mates. It was like something out of a film; our eyes met and…"

I could no longer hide my amusement at her rapture and she frowned.

"Oh I know what you're thinking" she said defensively.

I had to chuckle but I took her hand and squeezed it.

"I'm only thinking how good it feels to be young and in love; are you seeing him again?"

She seemed a little deflated at my words. "I don't know; I've given him my number but he hasn't rung yet."

"It's only early, he might still be in bed."

She brightened immediately. "Of course, I didn't think of that."

I watched her during the day as she nipped off to check her phone whenever she had a spare moment but I didn't need to ask because it was obvious from her manner that he hadn't been in contact. My heart ached for her; it was a long time since I'd been in the throes of first love but the agony that goes with it never leaves you.

When she came in on Sunday morning she seemed to be back to her normal self; I didn't ask if he'd phoned because she wouldn't have been able to resist telling me if he had. She seemed to have got over the disappointment anyway.

It was late in the afternoon when the two young girls almost burst through the front door. Sophie was setting up some empty tables ready for the next day but looked up when they came in. One of the girls hurriedly made her way through the tables and grabbed Sophie's arm.

"You'll never guess who we've just seen" she gasped.

"Elvis?" said Sophie.

"Don't be stupid. We bumped into them lads we met the other night."

I knew I was eavesdropping but I couldn't help it and saw Sophie's expression change.

"Was Ryan with them?" she asked

"Yes, they were all there."

Sophie pushed her towards an empty table. "Go and sit down and I'll get you a drink and you can tell me everything."

"We can't" said her friend, "We've no money."

"I'll treat you" said Sophie.

When she came to the counter I said "Why don't you take a break, we're not busy now; get you and your friends a drink on the house."

"Are you sure?"

"Yes."

"Thanks Harriet, you're the best."

Olive had not long since left and there wasn't much to do but I kept myself busy behind the counter, wiping down all the surfaces and putting what was left of the fresh produce into the fridge. I would take a couple of the cakes home for myself and Sophie could take the rest. They would be good for a couple of days but I wouldn't sell them in the tearoom as everything needed to be fresh daily.

It was nearly four o'clock when the girls left; I was in the kitchen emptying the dishwasher when Sophie joined me.

"That was Nina and Jade from school" she said. "They've been into Dunfield; that's where Jade lives and they've seen Ryan and his mates."

"Oh yes?" I said in a neutral tone.

"They said he asked about me and said he'd lost my number so they gave it to him again."

"There you are" I said, "I told you there'd be a good reason he hadn't been in touch."

She nodded. "Yes you did. Is it okay if I get off home now?"
"Of course."

I gave her her wages and said "I'll see you tomorrow."

It was the start of the schools' half term holiday and she was going to do some extra hours in the week. I was pleased that things had turned out right for her; there's nothing more painful than unrequited love.

Chapter Four

The ensuing week was a blur of americanos, cream teas and toasted teacakes as the weather did us proud and brought out lots of visitors. There was little time for idle chat but Sophie managed to tell us that Ryan had rung her and they were meeting up at the weekend.

Sophie's help proved to be invaluable as it freed me up to do some baking. There were some things I could make in advance and store in the freezer but scones especially were much better baked daily. I was in the process of taking a tray of custard tarts out of the oven when Olive popped her head round the kitchen door and I could tell by her expression that something was wrong.

"What's the matter?" I asked.

"Carrie's just been in with the post and she said the Misses Yardley have been burgled."

"Oh no!" I said nearly dropping the tray. "When?"

"Last night apparently when they were in bed."

"The poor dears, they'll be devastated."

Hilda and Rita Yardley were two of my best customers who popped in most days. They were identical twin sisters in their seventies; neither of them had been married and lived together in a cottage on the outskirts of the village. It had been their childhood home and having no other siblings they'd inherited it jointly when their parents passed away. They were such gentle souls and I hated to think of them feeling scared and vulnerable. Whoever had done this to them should be horsewhipped.

"I'll pop in after work" I said "and see how they're coping."

I hadn't much time to worry about it because the lunchtime trade began to pour in and I was kept busy for most of the day but before I left for the night I put a couple of cherry scones and some carrot cake in a box. I knew these were Hilda and Rita's favourites.

When I arrived at the cottage my heart sank. Even though it was still broad daylight the curtains were closed and I had a premonition of how bad things were. I had to knock on the door a couple of times before I got a response and then it was a small voice I could hardly hear through the wooden panels.

"Hello, who is it?"

"It's me Harriet, I've come to see how you are."

The door opened as far as the restraining chain would allow it and I got a peek at an eye swollen with weeping then it closed again and re-opened enough to let me in.

"Come in" said Hilda, who was the doorkeeper.

She ushered me into the living room and closed the door, locked it and replaced the chain.

Rita was standing in the living room and even in the gloom I could tell her eyes were also swollen

"I'm so sorry to hear about what happened" I said when Hilda joined us. "Was much taken?"

"We didn't have much that was worth anything" said Hilda "but they've taken things that were of sentimental value."

"Our grandfather's pocket watch and our mother's wedding ring" said Rita "and they've emptied the display cabinet."

I looked over at the mahogany framed cabinet which I knew was their pride and joy; it's glass shelves were almost bare.

"They probably thought that because we're old we'd have lots of antiques" said Hilda.

Rita went on "The only antiques in this house are us."

"They wouldn't get much for us though" said her sister "and we're not that easy to carry off."

I had to smile; even in what must be one of their darkest hours they hadn't lost their sense of humour.

"I take it the police have been" I said.

"Oh yes" said Rita, we've given them details of everything that's missing and they've dusted for fingerprints."

"But they didn't seem hopeful that we'd get anything back" said Hilda.

"Are you insured?"

"Well yes" said Rita "but the things they've taken are irreplaceable."

I stayed with them for a while longer ; Hilda put the kettle on and we shared the carrot cake I'd brought. When I left I heard the lock turn in the door behind me and the chain go on. I could understand their need for security but they'd told me that the burglars had come in through the kitchen window. The Police surmised they'd prised it open with something like a crowbar, damaging the catch; victim support had been and boarded it up for them but that was going to be another substantial expense on top of everything else. I hoped the insurance would cover it.

When she arrived for work the next morning Olive wanted to know how I'd got on with the Misses Yardley. I told her everything I knew and Sophie arrived in the middle of our conversation. She was also concerned.

"The news is all over the village" she said, "I've told Nan to be extra careful when she's locking up at night; I'm glad I'm staying with her because I think it makes her feel safer than being on her own."

"I know what you mean" said Olive, "having Norman with me makes me feel safer; I know he's not exactly Rambo but it's better than being on my own." She suddenly realised what she'd said and shot me an apologetic look. "I'm sorry Harriet, I didn't mean…"

"It's alright" I said, "I can look after myself."

In fact I hadn't thought about it at all before now and although I wasn't really worried I promised myself I would take extra precautions in future when I locked up.

I let it slip to the back of my mind as the cafe started to get busy and I was in the kitchen making up sandwiches for a customer when Sophie came in with a face like thunder; she banged the tray of pots she was carrying down by the sink.

"Careful" I said with a chuckle, "any breakages will come out of your wages."

"Sorry Harriet but Brad's just walked in and plonked himself at one of the tables."

I hoped there wasn't going to be any trouble. "Has he come to see you?"

"No, he says he's meeting someone."

"Well he's entitled to do that I suppose, cafes are places where people meet up and we haven't barred him."

"I wish we had! He says he's meeting a girl from college but why did he have to come here?"

I gave her a knowing smile. "To make you jealous? It seems to be working."

"It's certainly not" she said, "I couldn't care less."

I was expecting her to stamp her foot but she didn't.

"Tell you what" I said, "you take these sandwiches to the couple on table four and I'll take Brad's order."

"Thanks Harriet."

Brad was looking at the menu as I approached him; he looked up and seemed disappointed that it was me

"Can I get you something?" I asked.

"I'll just have a latte for now please; I'm waiting for a friend and we'll order food when she arrives if that's okay."

"That's fine." I said.

He's polite enough, I thought, and he seems like a decent lad but there must be something wrong to turn Sophie's family against him.

As I was serving his coffee the young lady arrived. She grinned broadly when she spotted him and came over to sit next to him at the table.

"I'll give you a few minutes" I said "and then I'll come to take your order."

Sophie was peeping round the kitchen door watching them.

"I thought you weren't bothered" I said when I reached her.

"I'm not" she said, "I'm just curious."

She flounced back into the kitchen and I turned to see Olive smiling behind me; she raised her eyebrows. "Not bothered at all" she said.

Sophie set about loading the dishwasher with the morning's dirty pots. Olive and I left her to it.

Brad and his friend ordered a round of sandwiches each and I noticed they seemed to have a lot to talk about. I also noticed that every now and again he would glance towards the kitchen but even when he came to the counter to pay the bill Sophie kept out of sight.

When they finally left I went into the kitchen. "They've gone; you can come out of hiding."

"I wasn't hiding" said Sophie as she wiped down the worktop nearest the sink, "I've been busy."

I wasn't convinced but I didn't press the matter, however, something puzzled me.

"Why don't your family like him? He seems like a nice lad to me."

She sighed. "It's a long story but his family are a bit dodgy for a start; both his dad and his elder brother have been in prison. When Mum found out she went ballistic and ordered me to stop seeing him."

I was about to say that it didn't mean that *he* would get into trouble but then thought how I'd feel if Sophie was my daughter.

"Well you've got Ryan now." I said in an attempt to cheer her up.

Her face brightened. "Yes I have."

Chapter five

When Sophie arrived for work on Sunday morning she was either in a dreamworld or as giddy as a kitten; Olive and I looked on with amusement although the dreamworld was becoming an obstacle to her usual efficiency. She'd been out with Ryan the night before; he'd taken her for a burger and then they'd sat and chatted until it was time to get the last bus home. By the look on her face I suspected they'd done more than chat. She'd given us the update as she was changing into her apron.

"Are you seeing him again?" I asked.

"Yes, next Saturday, he's taking me to the cinema."

"Aren't you seeing him before that?" asked Olive.

Sophie pulled a face. "No, he doesn't go out much during the week. He's up really early for work and so he goes to bed early."

"Where does he work?" I asked.

"I'm not sure; I think it's in the warehouse of one of the big supermarkets."

"Didn't you ask him?"

"Yes but he said he didn't want to waste time talking about work when there were better things to do."

Her face flushed red and she giggled; Olive jumped in straight away."

"I hope you're being careful."

Sophie flushed an even deeper shade of red.

"Olive! We only kissed nothing more; I'm not like that."

"I'm glad to hear it" said Olive. "You're a bright girl with a promising future ahead of you and you don't want to spoil it."

I knew Olive was only concerned for her and thankfully so did Sophie because she smiled and gave Olive a salute. "Yes ma'am" she said.

"Don't be cheeky" said Olive and Sophie swerved just in time to avoid having her bottom slapped with a tea towel.

At the end of the day I handed Sophie a nice fat pay packet and thanked her for her hard work during the week.

"I've enjoyed it" she said, kissing the pay packet "and I'll enjoy spending this."

Mondays were often one of our least busiest days so I told Sophie to take the day off; school had started back but as she'd completed her exams she didn't need to go back in. Olive was preparing sandwiches in the kitchen so I was on my own in the tea room when Irene Morrison came in for her elevenses. I could sense she wanted a chat and I surmised it was about Sophie so I called Olive in from the kitchen and sat down with Irene.

I was right about the chat but wrong about the subject.

"Have Hilda and Rita been in?" she asked.

"Not since the break-in" I said, "I think they're reluctant to leave the house."

"Nasty business that" said Irene, spooning a heap of sugar into her coffee and giving it a thorough stir. "Who'd do that to two old ladies?"

"They don't care what effect it has on the people they rob, do they?" I said, shaking my head. "Such people have no conscience."

"You're right." She took a sip from her cup. "It's unsettled me I can tell you."

"At least you've got Sophie staying with you."

"I know but it happened during the night and they never heard a thing."

"That's true but you have to try and put it out of your mind or you'll never get any sleep."

The door opened and two lots of customers came in; Olive was already serving someone else so I excused myself and went back to work.

Irene finished her drink and gave us a wave as she left.

I couldn't wait to get my shoes off when I got home; my feet felt as though I'd been walking on hot coals. I'd underestimated the amount of custom we'd have when I gave Sophie the day off but I couldn't expect the girl to work seven days a week. Olive and I had done it over previous holiday periods but we were both getting to an age where we needed to take time off as well. What was the use of a healthy bank balance if your body was too worn out to enjoy it. It was obvious we needed another member of staff.

I broached the subject with Olive before Sophie arrived the next morning.

"I don't know about you but last week really took it out of me, especially yesterday when there were just the two of us."

"Me too" said Olive, "when I got home last night I steeped my feet in some lovely relaxing foot wash I got for Christmas last year; it was heavenly."

"Well don't jump down my throat" I said, which made her brow crease with suspicion, "but I think both of us are getting too long in the tooth to be working seven days a week."

She shook her head. "I wouldn't have the energy to jump anywhere and in fact I said exactly the same thing to Norman last night."

I was relieved that she agreed although part of me felt terrible that I was working her too hard. "I've decided to advertise for another part-time member of staff for over the summer."

"That's brilliant but can the business afford it?"

"I don't think it can afford not to, otherwise both of us will be in early graves. Besides I've never aspired to be Alan Sugar or Richard Branson, as long as I can pay my bills and have a bit left over for a few of life's luxuries I'm content."

Olive nodded. "Well if you're sure, I'm not going to argue with you. Will you put a card in the window again?"

"Yes, I'll do it now."

It was Friday evening before I got a response to the card in the window; I was beginning to think I would have to advertise further afield but when an applicant finally did appear I wasn't sure how to react.

Sophie had left for the day and Olive was just about to get her coat when the door opened and Brad walked in and made his way to the counter. She gave me a look but then turned to serve him.

"What can I get you?"

"I was actually hoping to speak to Mrs Jones," he said.

I looked up from what I was doing and asked "How can I help you?"

"I've come about the job."

My heart sank to my boots but I managed to paint on a welcoming smile.

"Take a seat and I'll join you."

Behind his back Olive mouthed the words "Shall I stay?" and I gave her a brief nod.

I sat opposite him at the table he'd chosen and while I was trying to find the words to open the conversation he said "Look Mrs Jones, I know you might have been told some things to make you wary of me but I'm not a bad person."

The look on his face was so sincere that if he wasn't telling the truth he was a good actor.

"I like to make my own mind up about people," I said, "but the problem is if I employed you, how would you and Sophie be able to work together?"

"I've put all that behind me; I've accepted that Sophie and I are well and truly finished and I'm seeing someone else now."

"The girl you brought for lunch?"

"Yes, I'm sorry if it caused trouble I honestly didn't know Sophie would be working."

Again he seemed very sincere but I had my doubts.

"It would only be part-time" I said.

"That's fine. My mum's not in the best of health and Dad's - well let's say he's away a lot; I need to earn some money but I don't want to leave Mum on her own too long."

I wasn't sure if I was being sold a sob story but if I was he was doing a good job. We discussed rates of pay but I couldn't specify hours and times at the moment until I'd worked that out with Sophie and Olive. I might be being duped but I couldn't help liking the lad and in the end I said "Leave me your number and I'll get back to you as soon as I can. I have to take Sophie's feelings into consideration so let me talk to her. If she's okay with it then so am I."

"I understand," he said, "and I'm grateful that you're even considering it."

I stood to end the interview and gave him a warm smile. "I'll speak to her tomorrow and ring you afterwards."

He thanked me and said goodbye to myself and Olive before leaving and closing the door behind him.

I turned to Olive whom I knew would have been listening in. "What do you think?"

"I think Sophie's going to go mad but I actually took to him."

"So did I."

"Even so it could be opening up a war zone"

I had the same thought but there was nothing I could do until I'd spoken to Sophie.

Chapter six

"Would we be working together?" asked Sophie, when I told her about Brad.

"Yes, sometimes" I said. "The idea is that we can all have at least one full day off during the summer so there would be days when you'll be in together."

She tilted her head to one side; a habit I'd seen her use before when she was thinking.

"Despite what people say Brad is a decent bloke" she said finally, "I know he'll work hard for you and we've both moved on; I've got Ryan and he's with that other girl so it's fine with me if you want to take him on."

I smiled and put my hand on her shoulder. "I'll ring him later; he can come in tomorrow for a couple of hours and you can show him the ropes."

She nodded and went over to clear a table. Olive came up to me.

"Y'know you're the boss Harriet, you didn't really need to ask her permission."

"I know that" I said "but I believe in respecting people's feelings; it makes for a happier workforce."

"Er, I don't remember you asking my opinion in either case."

"That's because we're very good friends and I know we think alike."

"Do we?"

"Eventually" I said.

Brad was delighted when I rang him with the good news. He came in promptly, the following day, at the time I'd given him and was eager to make a good impression. He didn't take to it as naturally as Sophie had; I was surprised how shy he was with the customers but Sophie was enjoying her sudden promotion from lowest in the ranks and helped him along until he found his feet.

The problems I'd anticipated about them working together never materialised but Olive and I were both of the same opinion that despite having 'moved on' they still liked each other - a lot.

I decided to give Brad the same hours as Sophie on Saturdays which meant that Olive could have the day off which she greatly appreciated. It meant that she and Norman could spend more time together which was more important than the money. If all went well I would offer him the same hours on Sundays as well so that Olive and I could both have a day off at the weekend.

I noticed that neither Brad nor Sophie mentioned their respective partners while they were together but when Brad wasn't around Sophie kept me up to date with her romance which seemed to be going well.

"By the way" I asked her a couple of days later, "have you told your nan that Brad's working here?"

She pulled a face. "Not yet, I'm waiting for the right moment."

"Well we can't keep it a secret forever; she's bound to pop in sooner or later and it will be a shock."

"I know but I don't want her to get upset."

"Then let me tell her."

Sophie's face brightened. "Will you?"

"Yes and I'll do my best to reassure her that there isn't a problem."

"Oh thank you Harriet."

The opportunity came the following morning when Irene came in for tea and toast. Brad was only coming in at lunchtime, Sophie was in the kitchen and Olive was serving P.C. Richards at the counter. I took Irene's order to her table myself.

"Do you mind if I join you" I asked as I placed the tray on the table. I'd added a cup of coffee for myself.

"Not at all" she said with a smile, "it's ages since we've had a chat."

I arranged the contents of the tray on the table and then sat down before I began.

"I need to tell you something" I said.

"Oh." She was about to take a bite of toast but paused midway. "Is it something to do with Sophie? Has she done something wrong?"

"No, no not at all" I instantly reassured her "but I've taken on another part-time member of staff."

Her brow creased in puzzlement. "Why do you need to tell *me*?"

"Because it's Brad."

Her toast dropped to the plate and she looked at me in disbelief so I went on quickly.

"Before you say anything let me explain."

I told her how he'd applied for the job and why and that I'd discussed it with Sophie before employing him. "They work well together" I said "and there is no hint of them getting back together."

"I hope not" said Irene, quite sharply, "her mother would go spare."

"But why?" I asked, "I know his family have a dubious reputation but he seems a good lad."

"It's not just his family" she said. "When he was going out with Sophie, a girl in Ainsthorpe claimed he'd got her pregnant. He denied it but, well - where there's smoke…"

"I see" I said. I couldn't help but be a little disappointed in him but it was actually none of my business and had no relevance to his working in the cafe; I could now see, however, why Sophie's family were so against him.

"You weren't to know" said Irene, picking up her toast once again "and she seems to have found a decent lad now to take her mind off him."

I murmured in agreement but I wasn't so sure that Sophie *was* completely over him and I started to wonder if I'd done the right thing in employing him after all.

When Irene left I loaded the dirty dishes onto the tray and took them to the kitchen to be washed. As I passed the counter P.C. Richards stopped me. "Have you got a minute Harriet?"

"Of course I have Pete, just let me get rid of this tray."

When I came out of the kitchen he was waiting for me. "Is it something in particular?" I asked.

"Olive's been telling me you've given a job to Bradley Benfield."

"That's right, is there a problem?"

"No, not as such; the lad himself has never been in trouble but his dad and older brother have records as long as your arm. In fact his brother Darren is inside at the moment."

"I know about his family Pete, he told me himself, but until he does something wrong I believe in giving him a chance."

"I knew you'd say that" he said with a smile "but just be careful, especially with all these robberies at present."

"Has there been another one?"

"Not in this village but there was one in Dunfield last week and a couple of the farms have been broken into."

"Have they no idea who's responsible?"

"Not at the moment; they're being very careful to cover their tracks but they'll slip up soon enough and we'll catch 'em."

"Let's hope it's sooner rather than later" I said "but thanks for the warning."

When he left I was deep in thought. I'd meant what I said about giving Brad a chance and from what I'd seen of him so far I couldn't imagine him being involved in the robberies but my talk with Pete had reminded me to look in on the Yardleys; they'd almost become reclusive since their break in and I hadn't seen them for a while.

Chapter seven

It took a while for Hilda to open the door when I knocked and then only after I'd stepped back so that she could see me through the window. I was both shocked and upset by the change in the sisters since I'd last seen them; their hair looked unwashed and uncombed and their usually smart clothing was replaced by baggy sweaters and jogging pants that both looked like they were ready for the washing machine. They had always been house proud but now there was dust on every surface in the living room and clutter littered the floor. It was as if they couldn't be bothered with anything.

They greeted me warmly enough as if they were happy to see me but there was something missing as if their pilot lights had gone out and no amount of spark from the outside world could re-ignite them; they had always been my main source of village gossip but now they had nothing to share because they rarely left the house.

Rita immediately went to put the kettle on when she saw the cake box in my hand and I wondered if they were bothering to feed themselves properly.

"How are you managing for food?" I asked.

"We telephone our order through to the supermarket" said Hilda "and George delivers it in his van."

"But you used to enjoy your trips out to do your shopping."

Hilda looked towards the kitchen where her sister was making the drinks. "Rita doesn't like to leave the house unattended but gets nervous if she's left on her own for too long."

"How are you managing to get your pension?"

"Oh I go to the post office once a week but I'm not away long; I only draw out what we need because we don't want to keep money in the house."

Rita came in with the drinks and Hilda made room on the coffee table for her to set them down. She'd heard what Hilda had said and nodded as she played, nervously, with her hair which was now growing over her ears.

"I think you could both do with a trip to the hairdressers" I said lightly. "That's something you always enjoy; I could take you if you like."

"You'd have thought I'd offered to drive Rita to the guillotine by the way she reacted; she started to fidget uncontrollably and looked to Hilda with fear in her eyes.

"It's okay dear" said Rita patting her sister's hand, "Harriet was only trying to be kind."

She turned to me. "We've decided to let our hair grow; mother would never allow us to have long hair when we were young because she said we'd catch nits so we've decided to do it now that we can please ourselves."

I smiled as if I understood which I did but not the explanation they'd given me. My heart went out to these two lovely ladies who had previously been so young at heart but that was something else the thieves had robbed them of. I felt guilty because I couldn't wait to leave; the atmosphere in the house was so depressing. When I did say goodbye I told them to ring me if they needed anything and they promised they would.

When I left the house I felt as if a heavy load had been lifted from my shoulders and I felt guilty again. This couldn't go on; I was determined that Hilda and Rita Yardley were not going to wither away inside those four walls; I didn't know how I could stop it but I'd have a flipping good try!

I discussed the matter with Olive the next day. Sophie and Ryan were both in and we weren't over busy so I toasted two teacakes and we left them to it.

"I don't know what you can do about it" said Olive as she sat opposite me at one of the tables. "You can hardly drag them from the house, kicking and screaming."

"I know but I have to think of something." The anger was building up inside me. "If I could get my hands on whoever was responsible I'd…"

"You and most of the village" said Olive.

When P.C. Richards came in later, I decided to have a word with him to see if he knew of similar cases.

"I believe they've had visits from the victim support service" he said "but they won't let them in so there's not much they can do."

I thought about it for a minute. "I wonder if they'd let them in if I was with them."

"It's worth a try" he said, rubbing his chin; "I'll get you the number for Victim Support or better still I'll contact them so they know everything's above board. Am I okay to give them *your* number?"

"Of course, I'll write it down for you."

"Thanks for having a word with Nan" said Sophie when we were in the kitchen together after lunch. "We've talked about it and she's cool with the situation.

"I'm glad about that" I said "I don't like to think I've caused problems for anyone."

"Anyway" she said, "you'll get to meet Ryan tonight because he's picking me up from work."

"Oh lovely, are you going somewhere nice?"

"Just for a burger and then to the cinema. He's passed his driving test and he's borrowing his dad's car."

I felt a nip of apprehension. "How d'you think Brad will feel about it?"

She straightened her shoulders and looked me in the eye. "It's none of his business; he knows I'm in a relationship."

She picked up the tray of clean cups she'd been stacking and walked past me into the cafe and I thought it's one thing knowing about something and another having your nose rubbed in it. I hadn't much time to worry about it because a bus load of tourists came to the village and we were kept busy for the rest of the afternoon. It was only as it neared the time for Sophie to finish that I remembered and I still wasn't as convinced as Sophie was about Brad's feelings but I came up with a solution. I found him washing up in the kitchen.

"You may as well go home now Brad; there's not much left to do."

"Are you sure? It's only quarter to."

"Don't worry I'll pay you until four but you've worked hard today and deserve an early dart."

He looked over at Sophie who was wiping down the coffee machine.

"You go early tonight" I said "and Sophie can have the early finish next time."

That satisfied him. That's okay then, thanks Harriet."

"I know why you did that" said Sophie, when he'd gone "but I told you he'd be fine about it."

"I don't know what you mean" I said, giving her an innocent smile.

At ten past four there was still no sign of Ryan and Sophie was starting to get fidgety.

"He's probably stuck in traffic" I said.

Sophie looked at me and nodded but then went to sit by the window to watch for him. Suddenly she jumped up and shouted "He's here, I'll introduce you."

The young man was hardly through the door before he apologised. "I'm sorry I'm late, I got stuck behind a tractor."

I gave Sophie an 'I told you so' look and she giggled.

"Harriet, Olive, this is Ryan."

We both shook hands with him. "Pleased to meet you Ryan" I said.

"Me too" he said, flashing me a charming smile.

I was impressed. He had what my mother would have called 'matinee idol good looks' with a mop of dark brown hair which curled slightly at the nape of his neck and behind his ears. . He was quite a bit taller than Sophie which wasn't saying much because she was so petite.

Olive and I waved them off as they left the cafe arm in arm. I gave a deep sigh; suddenly feeling very middle aged and on the shelf until Olive broke into my thoughts.

"Don't you think he has a look of someone?" she asked.

"Pierce Brosnan?"

"No you fool. Someone a little closer to home."

I looked at her for a moment until the penny dropped. "Of course, Brad."

"I thought so too" said Olive, "the minute he walked through the door.

"You're right" I said, "he's a bit taller than Brad but they could almost be brothers."

"You don't think they are" said Olive,"and Sophie doesn't know."

I shook my head. "I think Brad only has one brother and Pete Richards told me he's in prison at the moment. Besides they must have different surnames or Sophie would have said something."

"Well, Brad's dad is a bit of a rogue so it could be t'other side of t'blanket as they say."

We both started to laugh. "Listen to us" I said, "the Holmes and Watson of Overdale."

"Well I know my place" said Olive, "so come on Sherlock, let's get tidied up and then we can go home."

Chapter eight

The next morning the weather was overcast and the black clouds threatened to burst at any moment but the Toasted Bun Tearoom was bathed in brilliant sunshine thanks to a certain Sophie Morrison. Her smile lit up the building like a beacon in the gloom. She'd obviously enjoyed her date with Ryan. Her happiness was infectious and even Brad, who was oblivious to the reason, was touched by it."

"You're in a good mood this morning Sophe, did you win the lottery last night?"

"Sort of" she said, lowering her lashes and blushing.

If Brad suspected anything from her reaction he didn't show it other than to cease whistling the merry tune he'd been driving us mad with all morning. It was only when Sophie and I took a break together later that her ecstasy finally burst it's banks and she told me about her date.

"He was absolutely wonderful" she said "he treated me to burger and chips and then paid for me at the cinema: he even bought me some popcorn and a drink. I felt like a queen."

It was a sign of the times I supposed that girls expected to pay their own way on a date these days. "What film did you see?"

"Erm it was something soppy, I can't remember the title."

"Or much of the film I expect" I said, giving her an overstated wink.

She blushed a very deep red and then giggled. "Not a lot" she admitted.

I laughed. Some things don't change then.

I restrained myself from asking the question that was uppermost in my mind as it was none of my business after all but I did send up a private prayer that she was being 'careful'.

It was late the next day when I got the phone call from the victim support service. The woman, who introduced herself as Kate Parsons, apologised for the delay in getting back to me but they had been inundated with referrals due to the high number of burglaries in the area. During our conversation I said I would visit the Yardley sisters and see if they would agree to a visit if I was present and then I would ring her back.

The sisters were still cautious about opening the front door but were pleased to let me in when they saw who was calling, especially as I hadn't come empty handed. While Hilda poured the tea into the china cups, Rita brought out some small plates for the cakes.

I waited until we'd eaten before I brought up the main reason for my visit. When I mentioned a possible visit from the lady from victim support Rita was immediately on the defensive.

"It's very good of you Harriet but we're not letting strangers into the house at the moment."

"She'll have a badge to prove who she is" I said.

Rita was adamant. "How do we know it's real though, she might have made it herself or stolen it." She was starting to become quite agitated.

"What if I was to come with her?" I suggested.

The sisters looked at each other and Rita shook her head but Hilda seemed more willing.

"Harriet wouldn't bring anyone into our home if she didn't trust them, Rita."

Rita looked at me. "I know you wouldn't but I'm still not happy about it."

"She only wants to help you," I said.

Rita looked at Hilda who took hold of her hand. "Why not let Harriet bring this lady to see us and if it becomes too distressing for you we'll ask her to leave."

It took Rita a while to answer but eventually she nodded her head and said "Alright if you think it's for the best but you *will* stay with us while she's here, won't you Harriet?"

"Of course I will. Shall I make an appointment?"

After one final check with Rita, Hilda said "Yes please."

I rang Kate the following morning.

Kate called for me at the tea room and we walked round to the Yardleys' house together. I'd arranged a late afternoon appointment and left Olive to close up when the last customers left. As we walked Kate told me how busy they'd been during the recent crime wave. Her area covered Overdale and the neighbouring villages of Dunsfield, Ainsthorpe and Wallington. Under normal circumstances such a wide reaching patch would have been no problem because there was usually very little criminal activity but in the past few months she and her colleagues in other areas had been kept really busy.

"Do you think it's an organised gang?" I asked.

"I don't know about that but they do seem to know what they're doing because they seem to be picking their targets quite particularly."

"Yes, vulnerable people like Hilda and Rita!"

"It's not just private homes, they have targeted some businesses as well so be careful Harriet."

"I am" I said.

Hilda was in the window watching for us as we approached the cottage; I'd telephoned earlier to let them know what time we were coming so they could be prepared. When the front door opened Kate showed Hilda her badge and introduced herself.

"Come in" said Hilda, "Rita is waiting in the living room."

Rita was sitting on the edge of one side of the sofa and I could tell by the way she was fidgeting with the buttons on her cardigan that she was nervous. Hilda directed Kate and I to the two armchairs while she sat with her sister and held her hand.

Kate started by giving a brief outline of what help the victim support service could provide. She then asked if she could take a look around the house, inside and out to see what was needed. Hilda offered to escort her and I took Hilda's place next to Rita.

"She seems very nice," said Rita, who had started to relax a little.

"She is," I said, "and hopefully she'll be able to put things in place to help you feel more secure."

"I hope so; Hilda and I have hardly slept since it happened."

I didn't tell her but it was plainly obvious by the dark circles under both their eyes and their general unkempt appearance. Instead I tried to lift her spirits by bringing her up to date with some of the village gossip until Hilda and Kate rejoined us.

Kate sat down and spoke directly to Rita. "I've been telling Hilda that there are several things we can do such as window locks and security lights and a stronger chain on your front door but Hilda will give you the full details later."

Rita nodded to show she accepted each of these things but I could sense that she wasn't totally reassured.

"What about an alarm?" I asked.

Kate sighed. "Unfortunately our funds don't run to things like that but there is a grant that the ladies can apply for if their own income is limited."

I looked at the sisters. Obviously I didn't know the state of their finances and I didn't think it was my place to ask but Hilda helped me out.

"We don't have much in the way of savings and our only income is our pensions."

"Then we need to apply for the grant" said Kate, "shall I leave you the application forms?"

"Yes please" said Hilda "but we may need some help with them; neither of us are good with paperwork."

"That's not a problem; either myself or Harriet could help you fill them in."

"Would you do it Harriet?" asked Rita.

"Of course" I said, "we'll look at the forms and see what information you need to get together before we start."

"Shall I come back at the same time next week to collect them or will you post them?" asked Kate.

"We'll pop them in the post" said the sisters in unison.

"That's fine. In the meantime I'll start the ball rolling on those other jobs" said Kate.

"Will they have to come into the house?" asked Rita, starting to fiddle with her buttons again.

"I'm afraid so," said Kate.

"Will you come round and be with us Harriet?" asked Rita, her eyes pleading.

"Of course I will," I said with more cheerfulness than I felt. We were approaching the summer holidays which was our busiest period in the tearoom and I hoped I could spare the time. Thank goodness for Brad and Sophie I thought.

Chapter nine

We really were experiencing an upsurge in business. The weather had been glorious for the past couple of weeks and the forecast predicted it was to continue for the rest of the summer; again I sent up a prayer of thanks for my two extra members of staff.

The weekends were naturally the most busy so I decided that all four of us should work together but during the week we were each able to have a day off, Monday to Thursday.

Ryan sometimes came to pick Sophie up from work but he always waited until Brad had left before he made an appearance. I suspected that Sophie had suggested it to avoid any awkwardness but when it was Brad's day off he always came a little earlier for a drink and a piece of cake while he waited.

He seemed a really nice lad; he had lovely manners which is often quite rare these days and not only with the younger generation. He appeared to really care for Sophie who was besotted with him.

There was only one thing that bothered me. She'd started to make changes in her appearance. She'd dyed her hair a pretty shade of ash blonde and although it was still cropped quite short it no longer resembled a frightened porcupine at a fancy dress party but framed her face with natural waves. She was blossoming into a real beauty but I was worried that she was losing something of herself.

Her clothes had become more conventional as well and some of the piercings had been removed. "Ryan often comes shopping with me," she told me. "He likes to help me choose nice things."

Although the clothes he helped her choose were lovely and suited her, I couldn't help mourn for that feisty individual who had bounced into my tearoom some weeks ago. Brad had only made one comment in my hearing which was "You'll be taking up knitting next."

Olive had whispered in my ear. "I hope it's not baby clothes."

One morning Olive came in with some news.

"Norman's getting himself all excited; he's like a kid just about to go to Disneyland."

"Why?"

"He went to his fishing club last night and it seems that him and his cronies have entered a big match next week on some private estate; it seems the prize money is quite attractive."

Sophie and Brad overheard the news as they arrived for work.

"Oo Olive" said Sophie, "He might come back a rich man."

Olive laughed. "Oh love, my Norman's been fishing since he was a lad and I've never known him to catch enough in one go for a decent fish supper."

Brad took his apron from the peg. "I've not been fishing for ages; Granddad used to take me and my brother a lot until…"

"Until what?" asked Sophie.

Brad reddened. "Until the police caught up with him; it seems he didn't have a licence. Mum went berserk and wouldn't let him take us after that."

"Did he stop going?" I asked.

"Oh no, not Granddad; he said it was his right."

"How many times did he get caught?" asked Sophie.

"Only the once. He said having us kids with him had hampered his getaway the last time."

Brad managed to keep a straight face but the rest of us couldn't help but laugh.

We took up our positions in the tearoom as the first customers started to arrive. Olive and I were behind the counter and Brad and Sophie took orders and served.

"When is the match?" I asked Olive.

"Next Wednesday"

Brad was coming to the counter with an order. "That's my day off" he said. "If you want to go with him I'll swap with you."

Olive gave him a stern look. "Not likely; I did my share of sitting on the side of a canal watching him fish when we were courting."

Sophie joined us at that moment. "So Olive, when you'd landed the fish you were angling for you stopped going."

Olive giggled. "I suppose you're right. Good job he weren't a tiddler or I might have thrown him back."

"Olive!" said the three of us together but she just laughed.

I spent my next day off round at the Yardleys' cottage; the workmen had come to put in the new security locks but Rita had refused to let them in until I arrived and checked their identification badges. Hilda could have done it but I was becoming the only one whose judgement Rita trusted. It was a big responsibility on my shoulders.

Hilda told me that Kate had phoned to tell them their grant application had been approved and someone would be in touch to arrange for the alarm to be installed.

"I hope it won't be too complicated to set," said Rita.

"It won't be" I said, hoping I was right.

"We learned how to work the video recorder, didn't we?" said Hilda. "And that baffled us at first."

"Yes we did," admitted Rita.

"And the washing machine and the microwave" went on Hilda counting off the various appliances on her fingers.

"Yes we did" repeated Rita.

"We're only elderly Rita, not stupid."

That made Rita smile for the first time since I arrived. "Absolutely!" she said.

It didn't take the workmen very long to complete the jobs and they were all packed up and on their way by lunchtime. One of them had taken the sisters round the house showing them what they'd done and how things worked. I hope you'll feel much safer now" he'd said.

Hilda had given an affirmative but Rita said nothing.

"Will you stay for lunch?" asked Hilda when she'd closed the door on the workmen.

"I thought we might go out for lunch" I said with determined enthusiasm. "Why don't I drive you both round to the cafe and treat you to lunch for being so brave. I know Olive would love to see you. I'll bring you back afterwards."

Before Hilda could speak Rita said "I don't really feel like going out and besides I think Hilda has prepared something."

Hilda looked at her sister and then at me. "I did get a tin of ham when I ordered the shopping and the milkman delivered some fresh bread rolls this morning but they'll keep."

She looked back at Rita. "It might do you good to get out of the house for a while."

"I don't think so" said Rita, "I feel like I'm starting with a cold so I'd be better staying in."

Hilda looked at me and shrugged her shoulders.

"That's alright" I said, "a ham roll will be fine."

"There you are Hilda" said Rita, "Harriet would rather stay in as well."

It was no use arguing, she wasn't going to budge. "Shall I give you a hand in the kitchen Hilda?" I said.

"No Harriet, you're our guest." She gave her sister a pointed look. "Rita can help me - if her cold will allow it."

"Yes of course" said Rita, happy to have got her way. "You make the sandwiches and I'll put the kettle on."

I purposely hadn't brought any cake with me because I'd been determined to get them to the tearoom but Rita managed to find some biscuits and a pack of shop bought scones.

"They're not as good as yours" she said when she laid the plate on the coffee table "but we'll manage."

We ate lunch in an atmosphere of uneasy silence. Hilda was cross with Rita and Rita knew it but was intent on having her own way.

"Which one of you is the elder?" I asked in an attempt to change the mood.

"I am" said Hilda.

"Only by half an hour" said Rita.

Hilda looked sharply at her sister. "Yes but that half an hour made you the baby of the family and I was always expected to look after you."

Rita concentrated on picking some crumbs from her plate but said quietly "Which you know I'm grateful for."

It was the first time I'd seen the sisters at odds with each other and it saddened me beyond measure. Harmony was another thing the robbers had taken from them and it couldn't continue; I could see that Hilda was becoming increasingly frustrated with Rita and it was driving a wedge between them.

I was glad when the meal was over and I could politely take my leave but as I got up to go Rita said "You will come round when the burglar alarm men come won't you Harriet?"

"Yes" I said, "on one condition."

"What's that?"

"When he's finished you'll let me take you to the tea room for a treat."

"Oh I don't know, I ..."

Hilda put her hand on her sister's arm to stop her. "It's a deal." she said with emphasis.

Chapter ten

"Did Norman get off alright?" I asked Olive on the morning of the fishing match. She was in the kitchen preparing baguettes for lunch.

"Oh yes, the mini bus picked him up early this morning."

"What time will he be back?"

"Heaven knows; they'll end the day in some pub or other sharing tales of the ones that got away."

"Now you never know" said Sophie as she came into the kitchen with a tray of dirty pots. "He might come back with a bright shiny trophy and a pocketful of readyies to treat you with."

Olive looked up and pointed the buttery knife to stress her point. "If that happens I'll dance the fandango in my underwear to the top of Jedburgh Rd. and back."

Sophie laughed so much that crockery rattled dangerously on the tray before she safely laid it down by the sink.

"Now that I'd pay to see," she said.

"Well your money's safe" said Olive, returning to her task "because if such a miracle *was* to happen the cash will disappear behind the bar for him and his mates."

"But what about the trophy?" persisted Sophie.

"I'll wear it on my head all day tomorrow."

Sophie looked at me. "Do you think God'll listen if we pray hard?"

"Oh he'll listen" I said "but he doesn't always give us what we ask for."

"Just as well I suppose" she said with a sigh. "I don't think my laughter muscles could cope."

When Olive and Sophie had left for the evening I locked the front door and put up the closed sign then I went to empty the dishwasher. I quite liked these few minutes on my own in the shop which is strange because I'm on my own at home but I took my time putting the dishes away in their set places before collecting my bag to go home.

As I got to the car my mobile rang; it was Olive.

"Hello" I said, "did you forget to tell me something."

There was a short silence but when she answered I could tell something was wrong. She could hardly get her words out and it sounded as though she was crying.

"Oh Harriet, we've been robbed!"

I felt as though I'd been punched in the stomach.

"Oh no; have they taken much?"

"I don't know, I haven't had time to check but the house is a mess and Norman's not home yet."

"I'll be round straight away. Have you phoned the police?"

"Yes, they've told me not to touch anything until they arrive."

She wasn't joking when she said the house was a mess; drawers and cupboards had been opened and searched, their contents strewn all over the floor.

"Oh Olive" I said as I wrapped her in a fierce hug, "how did they get in?"

"They broke the kitchen window. I'm sick of telling Norman that we should have double glazing but he's such a skinflint."

"I'm no expert" I said, "but I don't know if even that would have kept them out if they were determined.

The doorbell rang, making us both jump. Olive unwrapped herself from my embrace and went to answer it. It was the police.

Two male detectives walked into the room, the older of whom made the introductions.

"Hello, I'm Detective Sergeant Evans and this is my colleague detective constable Mills. Do you mind if we sit down."

After inspecting the warrant cards they produced Olive indicated towards the three piece suite in the centre of the small room. "Not at all," she said. "This is my friend Harriet.

D.S. Evans started by asking general questions about who we were and who lived in the house and D.C. Mills wrote everything down in his notepad.

"So you say there's usually someone at home during the day?"

"Yes" said Olive, "I work at Harriet's tea shop but my husband is retired."

"But he wasn't at home today?"

"No, he belongs to the local fishing club and he's been out at a competition all day."

"It seems too much of a coincidence" said the D.S., "Who might have known that the house would be empty today.

Olive shrugged her shoulders and gave it some thought.

"Norman's friends at the fishing club, I suppose and I only told the people I work with at the cafe."

D.C. Mills looked up from his notepad. "Can you give me their full names please."

"You'd have to ask Norman for the names of his fishing friends."

"That's fine" said the D.C with a smile, "what about your work colleagues?"

"There's only the four of us; myself, Harriet Jones, Sophie Morrison and Bradley Benfield."

The two detectives exchanged glances.

"Benfield, did you say?"

"Yes" said Olive, "I know you'll know his family history but Bradley's a good lad."

"Were all members of staff working today?" he continued.

My heart sank and I knew Olive was feeling the same because she struggled to get the words out.

"No, it was Brad's day off but I'm sure he wouldn't do anything like this."

The sergeant just smiled. "We'll have a word with him just to eliminate him from our enquiries. Now do you have any idea what was taken?"

Olive recited a list of the things she'd noticed were gone although she hadn't done a thorough search.

"There was a small amount of cash in the bedroom drawer and that's gone, Norman's best watch is gone and all of my good jewellery."

The D.C. wrote everything down and D.S. Evans said "The forensics team will be round as soon as possible. Try not to disturb anything until they've been and we'll be in touch as soon as we've got something to report."

I took the detectives to the front door and let them out. When I went back to the living room Olive was sitting in the armchair with her head in her hands.

"Would you like me to stay until Norman gets home?" I asked.

She looked up and the relief on her face was obvious. "I'd be really grateful," she said.

Neither of us had much of an appetite but I found some cheese in the fridge and made us both a sandwich with the bread I found in the cupboard. It was while we were eating that Olive asked "You don't think Brad had something to do with this do you?"

I gave a deep sigh. "From what I know of him I'd like to think not but then Ronnie Briggs didn't have 'train robber' stamped across his forehead, did he?"

"I think it would hurt me really badly if he had," she said.

"Me too." I said.

It was late when Norman arrived home and if he had partaken liberally of the demon drink he soon sobered up when he saw the state of the house.

"What happened here? Are you alright love?"

"I am now" said Olive, "thanks to Harriet, but oh Norman, what a mess it was in when I came back from work."

"Have they taken much? Have the police been?"

He took her in his arms as she tried to bring him up to date, her tears coming in floods again as she remembered.

I left them to it and made my way home. I was relieved to find everything as it should be but decided I needed to increase my own security measures.

Sophie arrived on time the next day and was surprised to find me behind the counter.

"I thought it was your day off," she said.

"It was but Olive won't be coming in today; she was burgled yesterday while she was here."

"Oh no, the poor thing!"

"I've told her to take as much time as she needs."

"Well I'll work extra shifts if you need me to."

"Thanks, that will help but if I know Olive she'll be back in no time."

Brad was late and when he did arrive he wasn't very happy.

"Sorry I'm late but I was in the police station 'til late last night and I overslept this morning."

Sophie was on him straight away. "What were you doing at the police station?"

He looked directly at me. "They think I had something to do with Olive's burglary but I didn't Harriet, honestly, you have to believe me."

"I do" I said and I meant it; he was either innocent or a really good actor.

"I wouldn't do that to anyone," he said, "let alone a friend."

"If it's any consolation" I said, "I don't think Olive believes you had anything to do with it either."

He seemed a little reassured but he wasn't his usual self for the rest of the day.

As I predicted Olive was back at work the next day.

"Are you sure you're okay to come in?" I asked.

"Yes I'm sure. Forensics have been and we've been able to tidy things up. The lady from victim support is coming round this afternoon, I think it's the one you know, but Norman's at home and he can deal with it. I'd rather be here."

"Have you heard anything from the police?"

"Not yet but I'm not holding my breath that we'll get any of the stuff back, even if they catch them."

"Are you insured?"

"Luckily, yes but some things are irreplaceable, aren't they?"

When Brad arrived for work the first thing he did was to protest his innocence to Olive and she reassured him that she believed him.

Chapter eleven

Because of Olive's speedy return to work I was able to take
time off to be with the Yardley sisters when they had their alarm
fitted and took the opportunity to have a chat with the workman
about an estimate for my own cottage. When he'd finished and
gone I reminded Rita of the deal we'd made.

"Yes Rita, you promised" said Hilda.

Rita stood her ground. "I don't believe I actually did Hilda, it
was you who promised."

"Oh Rita, come on" said her sister, "you must be sick and tired
of these four walls; I know I am and at least I've been going out
to the post office."

Rita looked as if she was going to cry. "I'm feeling a bit
poorly Hilda and I don't think I could eat anything anyway."

I thought Hilda was going to stamp her foot. "Well, you can
please yourself but I'm going."

Rita's face puckered. "But I really do feel poorly Hilda and
what if I have a funny turn while you're out?"

"If you're that poorly I suggest you go and have a lie down
and I won't waste my money bringing you back a cake."

A single tear rolled down Rita's cheek and I felt awful. "Don't
be mean Hilda." she said.

Hilda softened and took her sister's hands in her own. "I don't
want to be mean, love but I'm going stir crazy; I need to get out
more."

"Come on Rita" I said, "the cottage is more secure than Fort
Knox now and you also need to get out more."

Rita shook her head. "I'm sorry but I can't, not today. Perhaps
another time."

"In that case" said Hilda firmly, "I'll see you when I get back."

She almost pushed me out of the house and didn't look back as
we got into the car and drove off. She didn't speak until we
pulled up behind the tearoom and I realised she was holding back
her own tears.

"I feel awful for leaving her," she said, "but I don't know what else to do to get her to leave the house."

"Has she seen a doctor?"

She shook her head. "She won't leave the house to go and they don't make house calls unless it's an emergency."

"Perhaps you could go and see him on her behalf and explain."

"I'll see" she said and opened the car door to get out thus ending the discussion.

Olive greeted Hilda with open arms but didn't ask the obvious question when she saw me silently shaking my head.

"Let's get you seated" said Olive "and then I'll take your order although I think I can guess what it will be."

In the end Hilda relented and took a large slice of Lemon Drizzle cake home for Rita. I took her home but I didn't go in; I didn't think I could cope if Rita was in a state.

When Brad came in the next morning, Friday, he came to me with a request.

"I know Saturdays are busy Harriet and this is short notice but I wondered if it would be possible for me to finish after lunch tomorrow?"

"I'm sure that'll be okay," I said. "Are you doing something special?"

"A couple of mates are going to a gig in Manchester and they've offered me a spare ticket."

"That's quite a long way. Will you be back for your shift on Sunday?"

"Oh yes, no problem. We're going in Zak's car and we'll come back straight after the show."

"Well why don't you come in a little bit later on Sunday? You might need to lie in if you get back really late."

He looked like he was going to hug me but then changed his mind. "Thanks Harriet, I appreciate that."

Sophie must have been eavesdropping because I heard her say to Brad, "It's alright for some. I haven't been to a live gig in ages."

"You'll have to get what's his name to take you to one" said Brad in an offhand manner.

"I will" she answered using the same tone.

Next morning Brad was in bright and early and in a very cheery mood. In contrast Sophie, our usual ray of sunshine came in looking as if someone had taken her last sweetie and hardly spoke to us. It was the first time I'd seen her like this and I remarked on it to Olive when we were alone in the kitchen.

"I know" she said, "I was starting to fear for the cups and saucers the way she was throwing them into the dishwasher."

"Did you ask her what was wrong?"

"Yes and nearly got my head bitten off for my trouble."

"What did she say?"

"That nothing was wrong and she was fine."

Brad left us about one o'clock and Sophie's mood didn't improve. When there was a lull in custom I plucked up courage to try and engage her in what I thought would be a safe subject but I was wrong.

"Is Ryan picking you up tonight?"

"No."

The answer was short and to the point but I wasn't going to be put off so easily. I looked her in the eye.

"Right Miss sourpuss, while I'm wiping down the oven you can make me a latte and whatever you want yourself and we'll take a break and have a little chat."

She looked as if she was going to protest but then thought better of it and went to do as she was told. Olive joined in. "I'll have a pot of tea when I've finished putting these cups away."

Sophie was already seated at a table in the corner when Olive and I joined her.

"Right" I said, "are you going to tell us what's wrong and don't say 'nothing' because that's not true."

Sophie sighed and looked sheepish. "I'm sorry, I know I've been a grump all day and   I shouldn't be taking it out on you when It's Ryan I'm cross with."

"Why what's he done?" asked Olive and I in unison.

"He'd promised to take me out tonight but rang me this morning to say he was going camping with some of his mates instead."

"Couldn't you have gone with them?" I asked.

She shook her head and stirred the cream into her hot chocolate. "He said there was no room and that Nan wouldn't have let me go anyway."

"Well he was probably right about the latter," I said

"It's not like him to let you down, there must be an explanation," said Olive.

"He said it's been arranged ages and he'd forgotten."

"Perhaps that's true," I said.

"I know but I think there are some girls going."

"Oh I see" I said, looking at Olive for help.

Olive took a sip of her tea before saying "I can see why you might be upset; did you ask him about the girls?"

"He accused me of being jealous for no reason as they were all friends who'd been at school together."

"There you are then" I said.

She wasn't convinced and neither would I have been in her situation and at her age.

"Why don't you ring some of your own friends and arrange to meet up with *them*?"

"I have" she said, "I'm going round to Nina's; her boyfriend is going on the camping trip as well. Jade's meeting us later in Dunfield."

"Oh that's good" said Olive, "what will you do?"

"Probably go for a burger and then meet up with some other friends in the park."

"That's it, show Ryan you're not bothered."

"But I am" said Sophie, tears starting to well in her eyes.

"You know you are and we know you are but let him think that you're not."

A late customer came in for a takeaway coffee and Olive took the opportunity to leave the table while she served her.

"I'll clear these pots away" said Sophie with a loud sniff."

She pushed her chair back and started to load the cups onto the tray. She looked a picture of misery. Oh dear, I thought. The trials of young love. I didn't envy Nina and Jade one bit and it was a relief when she finally put on her coat and went home. Olive shook her head as she watched her closing the door behind her.

"I hope she's in a better mood tomorrow" she said.

"Me too."

We'd been rushed off our feet for most of the day, especially after Brad had left and as I watched Olive wiping down around the counter I could see she was shattered.

"Olive" I said, "why don't you get off home as well? I'll cash up and then I won't be long behind you."

Her body sagged with relief. "If you're sure, I don't mind waiting while you cash up though."

"No, off you go and get your feet up; I'll be fine."

When she left I locked the door behind her and set about cashing up the day's takings. It took me a while because we'd had such a busy day. I bagged up the money, putting tomorrow's float in a separate bag; sometimes I called at the night safe at the bank but I was too tired tonight so I put the two bags in the safe and checked it was securely locked before collecting my coat and handbag.

It was a lovely evening and as I made my way down the yard I decided I would have my supper in the garden with a glass of chilled white wine; I had some ready at home in the fridge. I unlocked the back gate and then remembered I'd left the piece of quiche I was planning to have with a salad for supper, in the cafe fridge so I nipped back to get it. As I turned the key to unlock the back door someone came up suddenly behind me and with a hefty shove pushed me through the half open door.

For a moment I was too disorientated to realise what was happening but when I managed to turn I could see there were two of them. I couldn't see their faces as they had crash helmets and masks on but one was quite tall and the other much shorter; it was he that did the talking.

"Open the safe!" he demanded.

"What?"

"I *said* open the safe!"

Some people might call it bravado , others stupidity but there was no way I was giving up my hard earned takings without a fight.

"I'll do no such thing" I said.

The taller one grabbed his friend's arm and pointed to my bag.

"Give me the keys" demanded the short one.

"No!" I shouted in his face.

He made a grab for my bag but I reacted quickly and swung it at his head, landing him a clout round the ear. The tall one came to his aid and tried to wrestle the bag from my hands but I clung on with all the strength I could muster. I saw the raised fist and felt the blow at the side of my head and then everything went blank.

When I came to my senses and slowly opened my eyes I was still dazed but I had the feeling that I was on the move. The rocking motion was making me feel slightly sick.

"Where am I?"

"You're in the ambulance Mrs. Jones" said a woman's voice, "we're taking you to the Royal Victoria hospital."

There was a hammer banging ten to the dozen in my head and when I tried to move, a sharp pain shot up my left arm.

"What happened" I said, every word making my head hurt more.

"You were attacked by robbers in your shop" explained the paramedic.

Memories started to make their way slowly through the fog in my brain. "Oh yes" I said weakly. "I think I remember, did they take anything?"

"I'm sorry I don't know; the police are there now and they'll come to see you when they've finished."

I tried to sit up but she stopped me. "Lie back and rest, Mrs. Jones. P.C. Richards found you when he was doing his rounds and sent for the ambulance but is there anyone you would like us to call?"

"No, not at the moment, thank you."

My family was too far away and I didn't want to worry Olive until I knew more. I tried to rest but every bump in the road rattled my aching body and it was a relief when we finally reached the hospital. The paramedics wheeled me on a trolley into the Emergency Dept. and I was taken straight into a cubicle. A nurse came to assess me fairly quickly.

"My" she said, "you're going to have a shiner in the morning. What happened?"

"I was attacked by two men who were trying to rob me."

"Oh dear, let's have a look at you. Can you tell me where it hurts?"

"Everywhere!" I said.

As it happened apart from the black eye, I'd mainly sustained only minor injuries. My wrist was badly sprained; I'd hit the floor with a bang when I'd blacked out but luckily nothing was broken.

The doctor, when he arrived, prescribed some strong painkillers and insisted I be kept in overnight for observation. Now perhaps it was time to ring Olive but I was too late; she already knew and came rushing in shortly afterwards accompanied by P.C. Richards. If I'd any illusions about the state of my face they were shattered instantly by the look on hers.

"Oh Harriet, what have they done to you?"

Once I'd assured her that I wasn't knocking on the pearly gates she stopped fussing and allowed P.C. Richards to speak.

"I hope you don't mind Harriet but I phoned Olive to come and have a look round to see if she could hazard a guess at what might have been taken."

" No, that's fine. What did they get?" I asked.

"Not that much really" said Olive, "the toaster's gone, the silver plated cake stand and a few other portables that they might be able to sell."

"What about my handbag?"

"We found that," said P.C. Richard's. "Olive's brought it.

"They've taken all the cash out of your purse" said Olive "but thankfully they left your bank cards."

"What about the safe keys, did they open the safe?"

"No," said P.C. Richards, "Your keys were still in your bag and you were slumped in front of the safe when I found you - guarding it 'til the last."

"Thank goodness for that" I said.

"I think they must have panicked when you went down and fled with whatever they could carry."

I suddenly thought of something and my good hand flew to my neck. "My locket!" They must have taken that off me while I was out of it and I've just realised my watch has gone as well."

"Were they expensive?" asked P.C. Richards taking out his notebook.

"The locket is nine carat gold, my husband bought for me on our first anniversary and the watch is a good one but it won't be worth a lot."

"D.S. Evans will come and see you tomorrow to get more details. I mainly came to bring Olive and see how you are."

"How did you find me?"

"I was doing my rounds and I noticed your back gate was wide open. I went in to investigate and saw the back door was open as well. I called your name as I went through it and there you were - out cold."

"It's a good job you did" said Olive "or she might have been there all night."

"Yes, thank you Pete."

"I was just doing my job but you take it more personally when it's a friend.

Before she left, Olive reassured me that the tearoom was in safe hands and she could manage fine with the help of Brad and Sophie.

D.S. Evans and D.C. Mills came to see me early the next morning. I'd just had breakfast; a bowl of cereal and a slice of toast and marmalade and was waiting, not too patiently, for the doctor to make his rounds and tell me I could go home.

"Good Morning Mrs. Jones" said D.S. Evans, "are you up to answering a few questions?"

"Yes, of course" I said.

I went through the whole episode, putting as much detail in as I could remember; I hadn't seen their faces and only the shorter one had spoken but I hadn't recognised the voice other than it was male.

"Had all of your staff been working yesterday?" asked D.C. Mills, pencil poised over his notebook.

"Yes but Brad left early, shortly after lunch; he was going to a gig in Manchester."

"That's Bradley Benfield, isn't it?"

"Yes" I said, feeling very uncomfortable but the sergeant didn't pursue the matter.

Pete Richards had passed on Olive's list of missing items and the forensic people had been in last night to dust for fingerprints. I was sure they wouldn't find any because both men had worn gloves.

Not long after the detectives had left the doctor came round and told me I could go home. The nurse had strapped up my sprained wrist and I was given a prescription for painkillers. My car was still parked behind the cafe but I was in no state to drive in any case. The nurse rang for a taxi for me and thankfully Olive had thought to leave me some money the night before so I was able to pay the driver.

My wrist was throbbing like mad by the time I let myself into my own living room so the first job was to take some painkillers but then I knew I couldn't put off ringing my daughter any longer.

"Hello Mum, I'm not used to you ringing at this time of day. Aren't you working today?"

"No love, I've had a bit of an accident."

"What kind of accident? Are you okay?"

Naiomi listened carefully and with unusual patience while I told her about the robbery.

"Right Mum, I'm coming up - no arguments."

"I wasn't going to argue" I said "but what about the children? "What about work?"

Naiomi was a secretary in a law firm and her husband was an accountant.

"I'm owed some time in lieu and Mike's working from home during the holidays so there's no problem."

"Well okay if you're sure; what time will you get here?"

"I'll try and get to you for about six thirty and I'll bring something for supper."

"Thanks love, I'll see you later."

I would consider myself a self- sufficient person who can manage perfectly well without help but I had to admit that the thought of Naiomi coming to stay with me made me feel much better.

The next thing I did was to ring Olive.

"How are you getting on?" I asked.

"We're fine. Brad and Sophie will help me out until you're fit."

"I don't know when that will be."

"Don't worry about it. I've told you we're doing fine."

"Have the detectives been in to see you?" I asked.

"Yes they came in this afternoon and spoke to us in turn but we couldn't tell them much."

I gave a sigh of relief. I'd had lots of time to go over things in my mind and had come to realise that both Olive and I had been robbed when Brad wasn't working and I'm sure it wouldn't have gone unnoticed by the detectives. I was still sure that he wasn't involved but was that because I didn't want to believe it? The taller of the robbers had fitted his build and he was careful not to let me hear his voice but surely he wouldn't have had the bare faced cheek to come into work with that on his conscience.

Naiomi arrived shortly after six but she wasn't alone; Yvette, her daughter, was with her.

"Hiya Nan" she said, throwing her holdall on the sofa, "I hope you don't mind me coming as well."

"Not at all, I'm delighted."

"She begged to come," said Naiomi "and I thought I would stop for a couple of days and then leave Yvette with you for a while."

Yvette was eleven years old going on thirty. "I'll be able to look after you" she said as she rushed over to squeeze me in an embrace. I let out a small cry.

"Careful love, that's my sore arm."

"Oh sorry, I'm not off to a good start, am I?"

"You weren't to know" I said after kissing her on the cheek, "and I'm sure you'll make an excellent nurse."

Naiomi had brought a homemade cottage pie that she'd had in the freezer.

"It'll have thawed out by now," she said. "I'll put it in the oven to warm up and by the time we've unpacked it should be ready to eat."

"That's lovely" I said. "I think I have some tinned carrots in the cupboard; we could have those with it."

"I'll do some shopping for you tomorrow Mum and get some supplies in."

"I'll come with you" I said and noticed the look on her face.

"It's only my wrist that's out of action, everything else is in perfect working order."

"Especially your tongue," she said, coming over to give me a hug. "As long as you don't overdo things; you've had a nasty shock."

I caught her hand as she moved away. "Whoever robbed the Misses Yardley stole their confidence as well and I'm not going to let them do that to me."

She came back and hugged me again. "I'd hate them forever if they did that" she said.

Although I was frustrated at being incapacitated it was lovely to spend time with my daughter and granddaughter. I wasn't used to being fussed over but I made the most of it and started to enjoy it. Yvette wanted to bring me breakfast in bed but I politely refused.

"I think I'll manage better at the kitchen table," I said.

I'd never been much of a one for breakfast, always preferring the extra few minutes in bed but while I had time on my hands it was good to spend time over coffee and toast with my two girls.

After breakfast, as promised, Naiomi drove us to the supermarket where I was able to stock up on some basic essentials and ingredients for meals for the next few days. When we got home I was instructed to make myself comfortable on the couch while Naiomi and Yvette packed the shopping away. Now *that* was something I *could* get used to.

It was while we were eating the cheese and pickle sandwiches that Naiomi had made for lunch that I plucked up the courage to say what was on my mind.

"I'd like to go to the tea room this afternoon, if that's alright."

Naiomi was mid-bite and had to wait until she'd swallowed before she could speak.

"I'm sure they're managing quite well without you."

"Yes, I'm sure they are but I'd like to bring the car back. I'm not happy about it being parked where it is for any length of time."

"How are we going to get it back? You can't drive yet."

"I thought we'd go down in a taxi and then you could drive us back in it."

Naiomi nodded as she took another bite. "Okay then, that's what we'll do."

"Oh good," said Yvette with delight. "Can I help in the cafe?"

"We'll see," I said, with a smile.

Chapter twelve

I could tell as soon as I walked through the front door that something was wrong. Every table was occupied and Olive and Sophie were rushed off their feet. When Olive looked up and saw me her face registered a look of great relief which was quickly replaced by one of concern.

"Harriet…" she started but I interrupted.

"Where's Brad? Is he in the back?"

She put down the tray she was about to load with dirty pots and took my arm, propelling me into the kitchen. "Brad's been arrested," she said.

"What! Is it to do with the robberies?"

"Yes, I think so. The police came here for him; luckily we'd only just opened so there were no customers. It was D.S. Evans and he said something about new evidence."

I felt as though my world had been knocked for six.

"I can't believe it" I said, "I just can't believe it."

Naiomi popped her head round the door. "It looks like you could do with some help out here. Have you got a couple of spare aprons for me and Yvette?"

Olive took two from the peg by the fridge.

"Thank you love, I'll be out in a minute" I said."

"I don't think so" she said, "you find yourself a seat and don't you lift a finger."

I rolled my eyes in Olive's direction. "I'm sure there's something I could do to help."

Olive patted me on the shoulder. "Do as you're told, woman."

I peeped round the door into the cafe. Yvette was enjoying herself, I could tell. She took her duties seriously and made it her job to clear the tables of dirty dishes and stack them in the dishwasher. She was a hit with the customers as well with her ever ready smile and cheerful conversation. She had so much confidence for an eleven year old but then so had her mother at that age. She hadn't inherited that from me; I'd been quite a shy child. No she was a chip off the paternal block that one.

When the rush was finally over and we were all able to sit down together for a break, the talk naturally turned to Brad.

"I can't believe it of him," said Sophie. "He's not like the rest of his family, he's a good bloke."

"Well the police wouldn't have arrested him if they didn't have good reason." said Naiomi as she stirred the contents of the teapot.

"No, Sophie's right love" I said, "I've got to know him quite well while he's been working here."

"But you see the good in everyone Mum."

"That's true," said Olive, taking a sip of her tea.

"Now Olive" I said, pointing my teaspoon at her for emphasis, "you liked the lad as well."

"Yes I did" she conceded, "that's true and if he does turn out to be guilty I'll be really upset that he deceived us like that."

Sophie put her hand over Olive's. "He's not guilty, you'll see. They'll catch the real culprits."

I hoped with all my heart that she was right.

"Well girls you really did me proud this afternoon" I said, as we sat down to our evening meal.

Naiomi had put a chicken casserole into the slow cooker before we left the house after lunch so all that was needed when we came home was to boil up some new potatoes and extra vegetables.

"I really enjoyed myself, Nan," said Yvette.

"Yes so did I" said Naiomi "but I didn't realise how tiring it can be; no wonder you're so fit Mum."

I poured myself a glass of water from the jug on the table. "It can be very tiring at busy periods like this afternoon but it's only hard work if you don't enjoy it - and I do."

Naiomi gave me her no nonsense stare and said "I've decided I'm going to ring work and apply for a few days of special leave so that I can help in the cafe until your wrist's better."

My first instinct was to say there was no need but clearly there was because Olive and Sophie couldn't manage on their own full-time.

"Are you sure?" I said.

"Positive and I'm sure Yvette will help as well, won't you darling?"

"Yes please."

I had to admit it was a load off my mind but it brought Brad back into my thoughts. I'd certainly had misgivings about taking him on in the first place but I'd come to like and trust him and I'd always believed myself to be a good judge of character; it would come as a heavy blow if he was guilty."

When we'd finished eating, Yvette collected the plates from the table and took them to the sink.

"You've got her well trained," I said with a smile.

"As you did with me and Vincent," said Naiomi. "By the way have you let him know about your attack?"

I felt a bit guilty. "No I haven't; do you think I should?"

"Well there's nothing he can do but he is your son and he might be upset if you don't tell him."

"Alright, I'll do it later."

"Now you go and sit in the living room" she said, "and I'll make us a coffee when we've washed up."

I wasn't used to this. "Are you sure there's nothing I can do to help?"

"Yes there is. Go in the living room and get out from under my feet."

I chuckled.

"What's so funny?" asked Naiomi.

"Nothing" I said, "I just wondered when it was that *you* turned into *my* mother."

Before I could make it to the armchair there was a knock on the door. "I'll get it," I shouted.

D.S. Evans and D.C. Mills stood on the doorstep.

"Good evening Mrs. Jones" said the D.S. "May we come in and have a word."

"Yes of course" I said, leading the way into the living room.

I invited them both to sit down. "Would you like a cup of tea or coffee?"

"No, thank you very much" said the sergeant, "we've just called to update you on the situation."

They sat on the couch and I took the armchair opposite. Naiomi, having heard everything from the kitchen, came and sat on the arm next to me.

"This is my daughter," I explained, "she and my granddaughter are staying with me for a while."

The two officers smiled and nodded a greeting before D.S. Evans said "We arrested Bradley Benfield this morning on suspicion of burglary."

"I believe so" I said, "what makes you think he's involved?"

"Some items reported stolen in an earlier robbery were found at his home."

"Fingerprints?" I asked.

"Unfortunately they'd been wiped clean."

Naiomi put her arm around me which gave me some comfort.

"Anyway" said the detective, "he's been released on bail on condition that he doesn't approach the cafe, yourself or any other member of staff."

"I understand," I said.

The officers stood to leave. "We'll keep you informed."

"Thank you" I said with a heavy heart.

Naiomi stood and led them to the door. "I'll show you out" she said.

Yvette, who had been eavesdropping, came out of the kitchen and took her mother's place beside me.

"Does this mean they've caught the man who hurt you, Nan?"

"I hope not love, I really hope not."

I insisted on going to the tearoom with them the following morning.

"I promise I won't lift a finger" I said "but I'll go mad sitting here all day on my own."

"Alright," said Naiomi "but I'll be watching you."

When she turned away from me I pointed to my eyes with my index and middle fingers and then pointed them at her. Yvette giggled but fortunately her mother had headed off to the bathroom and didn't hear.

"You *are* naughty, Nan"

"I know"

We both laughed.

Chapter thirteen

Olive had also had a visit from the detectives; unfortunately none of the recovered items were hers but I could tell she was starting to have suspicions that Brad was the culprit.

"I don't want to believe it Harriet but…"

"I know, I feel the same."

I decided that as I wasn't allowed to help in the tearoom I would walk round to the Yardley's cottage to see if they had any news. Hilda must have seen me coming up the path because the front door opened before I could knock.

"Oh Harriet, how are you?" said Hilda. "I heard about what happened when I went to the post office yesterday."

She went to hug me but then noticed my sling and thought better of it. "Were you badly hurt?"

"Not really, it could have been a lot worse."

She stood back to let me pass. "Come in and sit down." She called up the stairs. "Rita we have a visitor, Harriet's here."

I heard the sound of heavy footsteps plodding down the stairs and then Rita appeared. Her welcoming smile froze on her face when she saw me.

"Oh Harriet, you poor love, sit down and I'll put the kettle on. Are those cakes I can see in your bag?"

"Of course" I said, "I wouldn't dream of coming empty handed."

While Rita was in the kitchen, Hilda spoke to me in little more than a whisper.

"The incident with you has set her back a bit and she's still refusing to leave the house."

I answered her in a similar voice. "Oh no, what a shame. When I'm finally recovered we'll have to put our heads together to make a plan."

"What are you two whispering about?" said Rita who had appeared in the doorway.

I felt my cheeks go warm and Hilda blushed.

"Nothing dear, nothing at all."

I could tell by the look on her face that Rita didn't believe her but she let it pass.

"Have you told Harriet our good news Hilda?"

"Not yet, I was just going to."

I looked at her expectantly.

"We've got mother's clock back."

"Your mother's clock?"

Rita placed the tray of drinks on the coffee table. "The one that was stolen in the robbery."

"Well we've not exactly got it back yet" said Hilda, "the police have to keep hold of it because it's evidence but at least it's been found."

"That's wonderful news" I said with as much enthusiasm as I could muster, suspecting as I did where it had been found.

"Yes" said Rita "*and* they've arrested someone for the robbery."

I didn't tell them what I knew because I couldn't bring myself to speak it out loud so I painted on my brightest smile and celebrated with them.

"Does this mean you might pluck up the courage to come to the tearoom Rita?" I asked, trying to change the subject.

A worried frown creased her brow. "Er, not yet - but soon-perhaps."

I glanced at Hilda who gave an almost imperceivable shake of the head.

Despite rarely leaving the house herself, Hilda had somehow managed to soak up most of the village gossip which she delighted in passing on to me as we ate and drank. I stayed for an hour or so but the atmosphere in the house was still quite depressing which was the last thing I needed at the moment and it was like taking a blanket from over my head when I stepped out into the open air.

I took my time walking back to the cafe; it was a pleasant day to be out. The sun was shining strongly but there was a slight breeze to take the edge off its heat. It wasn't often I had the leisure to take advantage of being outdoors during the day and I was in no hurry to confine myself to four walls again.

I decided to take a stroll down the main street and browse along the shop windows, again something I rarely had the chance to do. Mr. and Mrs. Jameson ran the small supermarket that catered for most of the basic needs of the village and surrounding holiday homes and campsites. I paused outside the door to decide whether or not I needed anything when a middle aged woman carrying two bags of shopping nearly bumped into me as she came out.

"Sorry" I said, "I was in another world."

The woman looked hard at me before she said "You're Harriet Jones, aren't you?"

"Yes" I said. I didn't recognise her but then so many people came in and out of the tearoom and you only tended to remember the regulars.

The woman put down the shopping bag in her right hand and held it out to me. "I'm Kathleen Benfield - Bradley's mother."

I shook the proffered hand but felt uncomfortable. "Oh" I said, "pleased to meet you."

She gave a deep sigh. It's good of you to say so but I'm sure I'm one of the last people you want to speak to. I'm at my wits end with worry."

Her face, so much like Brad's that I should have guessed she was his mother, looked so downcast and far from being annoyed that my heart went out to her.

"You look worn out" I said, "why don't we go over to the tearoom and have a chat over a coffee."

She hesitated. "Oh I don't know…"

"Come on, I know the owner, we'll get it on the house."

"Are you sure?"

Without speaking, with my good hand, I picked up the shopping bag she'd put down. "Let me help you with this."

All four of my 'staff' looked at me in surprise when I escorted my guest through the door but I suspected that only Sophie knew her identity. Naiomi came over to me but I didn't enlighten her. Instead I turned to Kathleen. "What would you like to drink?"

"A latte please."

I turned back to Naiomi. "Make that two please."

The cafe was busy as it was almost lunchtime so I took Kathleen into the kitchen where we could talk in peace. I pulled up two chairs to the small table where we sometimes ate our lunch and Naiomi brought in the drinks.

"Thanks love" I said, ignoring the inquisitive look on her face.

She took the hint and went back into the shop and I turned to Kathleen. "We can be more private in here.

She played with the spoon on her saucer for a moment and then she looked me in the eyes. "I know you might not believe me but our Bradley is a good lad."

I thought for a moment and then said "I do believe you."

That took her by surprise. "Really?"

She visibly relaxed. "He's not had the best of upbringings with a father in and out of prison and our Darren's not much better but Bradley's different. I've done my best to steer him in the right direction."

"Where's Bradley now?"

"At home, moping around. He's devastated because he *is* innocent, I promise you. I don't know how that stuff got into our shed but I'm sure Bradley didn't put it there."

She took a deep breath and I could see the tears glistening in her eyes. "Our Bradley thinks the world of you and Mrs. Parker; he would *never* do anything to hurt the two of you even if he was a thief, which he isn't."

"I can't believe it of him either" I said, meaning every word. "I consider myself a good judge of character and if his bail didn't forbid it, he'd be welcome back."

"Thank you so much," she said. "It will do him good to know that."

"Give him my love when you get home."

"I will," she said, standing up "but I'd better be going now."

"You haven't finished your coffee."

"I'm sorry, it was lovely but Patrick, my husband will be wanting his dinner and he get's grumpy when he's hungry."

I wondered if I should read between the lines of that statement but decided it was none of my business; I had enough to contend with at the moment. She was hardly out of the door before Olive was at my side; she sat down in the seat vacated by Kathleen Benfield.

"Sophie said that was Brad's mother."

"Yes it was. I met her outside the supermarket."

"What did she want?"

"To plead Brad's innocence" I said.

"Well she would, wouldn't she?"

"But I believe her, Olive. There must be some other explanation."

"I want to believe he's innocent as well, Harriet but..."

She didn't finish the sentence, she just stood up and walked back into the cafe with her head down.

Once again I silently cursed whoever was responsible for these robberies; their actions had knocked the stuffing out of all of us in one way or another.

I picked up the cups from the table and took them to the sink. Sophie came in and after pouring the dregs down the drain she put them in the dishwasher.

"Right, that's a full load" she said, shutting the door and setting the cycle.

"You seem in a good mood" I said. "Have you made up with Ryan?"

She gave me a sheepish grin. "Sorry about the other day but yes we're friends again."

"Did he enjoy his camping trip?"

"I didn't ask him," she said haughtily, "because I didn't want to hear that he did. Anyway he's taking me out tonight."

"Somewhere nice?"

"I think so. My friend Nina is going out with his friend Vernon and it's her birthday today; the boys are taking us out for a meal."

"How lovely."

Before I could say anything else Yvette came in with a tray of dirty pots. "Olive said to tell you she needs you in the cafe Sophie."

"Oh right, I'd better get my finger out then" she said with a smile.

Yvette put the tray down on the worktop. "Mum says you and I could have our lunch Nan, shall I make us some sandwiches?"

"Yes love, that would be lovely; have a look in the fridge and see what we've got for a filling. You choose and I'll have what you have."

She went over to the fridge. "What about Tuna mayo?"

"Lovely" I said "and we'll treat ourselves to a piece of cake as well."

It was late afternoon when Sophie had a very excited visitor. I was sitting at one of the tables in the cafe, reading a magazine; Sophie was wiping down the counter and the cool shelves. The door burst open and her friend Nina dashed through it.

"Hello" said Sophie, "Happy Birthday."

Nina was positively glowing. "Thanks Sophe, I've just been out for lunch with Vernon and he gave me my birthday present so I can wear it tonight. It's absolutely gorgeous."

"Let's have a look."

Nina leaned forward but she had her back to me so I couldn't see what it was.

"It's beautiful" said Sophie. "It looks like real gold; it must have cost him a fortune."

"I know, he said he's been saving up for ages."

"Why don't you go and sit with Harriet and I'll buy you a birthday cappuccino."

Nina made her way towards me, her face one big smile.

"Come on then" I said, putting down my magazine. "Let's have a look."

When she held out the locket for me to admire my smile froze.

"Isn't it beautiful?" she said.

The lump in my throat nearly cut off my power of speech because the locket she was showing me was identical to the one I'd had stolen.

"Yes it is and it's very unusual," I finally managed to say. "Where did he buy it?"

"He didn't say but it must have been expensive, don't you think?"

Sophie came over with the coffee and I said "Why don't you sit with Nina for a few minutes and I'll see if I can help in the kitchen."

Naiomi was behind the counter and her face was troubled. "Are you okay Mum, you look as though you've seen a ghost."

"I think I have, sort of."

She followed me into the kitchen where Olive and Yvette were emptying the dishwasher.

"What's the matter?" asked Olive.

I sat down at the kitchen table and said "I'm sure I've just seen my locket - the one that was stolen."

"Where?" the three of them said in chorus.

I told them about Nina's gift and Naiomi wanted to go straight out and snatch it from around her neck.

"No, no, you can't do that" I said, "we have no proof. I'm going to ring D.S. Evans."

Luckily Sophie was completely unaware of my suspicions and it was agreed not to mention them in front of her and by the time the detectives arrived she'd gone home.

"I'm sorry Mrs. Jones but we will have to interview the girls and this Vernon character; you say you don't know his surname."

"No" I said, "but he's a friend of Soiphie's boyfriend, Ryan."

"Do you have a surname for Ryan?"

"No, I'm sorry I don't." I was beginning to feel a bit stupid.

"Not to worry" said D.S. Evans, "we'll go and see Sophie first; do you have her address?"

Thankfully that was something I could help him with.

Chapter fourteen

I was a little apprehensive about seeing Sophie the next day; with hindsight I wished I'd told her about the locket after Nina had left. When she arrived for work it was obvious that she felt the same; at first I thought she wasn't going to speak to me but when she caught me on my own in the kitchen she broached the subject.

"Don't you trust me Harriet?"

"Of course I do."

"Then why didn't you tell me about the locket?"

"Because I wasn't sure. No, that's not true. I was certain it was mine but I had no proof and I thought it was best to speak to the police first."

"They came to see me" she said.

"And?"

"I was able to give them Nina's name and address but I don't know Vernon's surname."

"Did they ask about Ryan? I told them Vernon was his friend."

"Yes, I told them Ryan's surname is Calderbank but I don't know his address, only that he lives in Dunfield."

"I'm sure Vernon bought it in good faith" I said, putting my arm around her shoulder, "but if he tells the police where he got it, it might lead them to the thieves."

Sophie nodded. "I've spoken to Nina and she said they've taken the locket away as potential evidence, she was really upset."

"I'm sure she was. I take it you didn't go out for the birthday meal."

"No, Ryan rang me and cancelled."

"I'm sorry."

Sophie looked straight at me. "What made you so sure that the locket was yours? It could have been one just like it."

I shook my head. "My husband's friend was a jeweller and he made it especially in the shape of a diamond because that was my maiden name. He always joked that he'd found a diamond when he met me. There was even a diamond engraved on the back."

"I'll tell Nina that" she said.

We were just finishing supper that evening when the detectives paid me a call at home.

They said they had Vernon in custody because they'd obtained a warrant to search his home and found more stolen items including my watch.

"What about his accomplice?" I asked.

"He refused to name him," said D.S. Evans "but Bradley Benfield is in the clear. We checked his whereabouts on the day and time you were robbed and we have eye witnesses to swear he was where he said he was.

"What about when Olive was robbed?"

"He has a cast iron alibi for that as well."

"I can't tell you what a relief that is," I said.

Naiomi was sitting next to me on the couch and she took my hand.

"I'm so pleased for you Mum, I know you trusted him even if I had my doubts."

"You don't know him like I do," I said.

When the detectives had gone Naiomi said "Well it looks like I might be redundant at the tearoom now, if Bradley can come back."

"Are you sorry?" I asked.

"Not Particularly, it's flippin' hard work."

We both laughed but Yvette had a sad face. "Does this mean I'm redundant as well?"

"Do you want to be?" I asked.

"No, I love it. Please can I stay on?"

I looked at Naiomi expectantly as I thought out a plan.

"You could go home to Mike and Tom and Leave Yvette here for a while. My wrist still isn't completely better and I would welcome the help."

"*Please* Mum, please say yes."

Naiomi smiled. "Okay then, you can stay for a few more days but I'll be glad to get back to my own job for a rest."

It was decided that Naiomi would stay for one more day so we could spend some time together that didn't involve work and I rang Brad to see if he wanted to come back to work.

He jumped at the chance to start the next day so I rang Olive to bring her up to speed. She was as relieved as I was that Brad was innocent.

The girls and I spent a lovely day together the next day. Naiomi drove us out to Bowness where we did lots of touristy things such as a sail around the Islands in the lake and paid a visit to the Beatrix Potter museum where Yvette bought herself a cup with a picture of Peter Rabbit on it with her 'wages' from the tearoom.

"I'm going to leave it at your house Nan, so I can use it whenever I come to visit."

"What a good idea" I said.

The weather was being really kind to us that day; the forecast showers had not yet made an appearance and we were able to sit in the sunshine and enjoy an ice cream. We found an empty bench by the side of the lake which was probably a mistake as we were immediately surrounded by greedy ducks all wanting to share our cones.

We ended the day with dinner in a restaurant on the main street. It was my treat to thank the girls for their help. My wrist was still a little tender but it was on the mend and I now felt I would be able to drive short distances.

Naiomi left the following morning, straight after breakfast; it meant she would be able to spend the weekend with Mike and Tom before going back to work. Before she went she gave Yvetter her instructions.

"Don't let your nan overdo things. I know she'll be back at work as soon as my back's turned."

"I *am* in the room" I said.

"I know you are Mum, and I also know I'm wasting my breath telling you to rest."

"Then don't waste it" I said, giving her a tight hug and a smacking great kiss on the cheek. "Save it for the boys when you get home."

We waved until the car was out of sight and then Yvette said "Are we going to the cafe Nan?"

"Of course we are," I said.

I parked my car in my usual space by the back gate which was now securely padlocked after the robbery. Rather than search in my bag for the key we walked round to the front door. Brad was serving a couple who were sitting at a table by the window and saw us approach. He opened the door and greeted me with a face splitting smile.

"It's so good to be back Harriet and it's so good to see you."

"It's really good to see you as well" I said, "and we're *all* pleased to have you back."

I introduced him to Yvette who blushed when she shook his hand. She's growing up I thought.

Olive greeted me with a similar smile but there was no sign of Sophie.

"I've sent her to work in the kitchen" said Olive, "she's got a face on her that would frighten the dogs let alone the customers."

"Why what's wrong?" I said.

"Boy trouble again. He stood her up and hasn't been in touch."

I went into the kitchen to get aprons for myself and Yvette. Sophie was at the worktop making up baguettes for the lunch trade. She looked up briefly when she heard me come in but then silently continued with her task. I kitted Yvette out with an apron and then sent her back into the tearoom before I spoke to Sophie. When she finally turned to look at me I could see the wet tracks on her cheeks.

"Is that the onions" I asked, pointing to her face, "or do you want to tell me what's wrong."

"No" she said, "I mean no it's not the onions, it's Ryan."

"Olive said he'd stood you up."

She nodded. "When I tried to ring him, his phone was switched off."

"Perhaps his battery was dead."

"I tried again and again but it was the same."

"I expect there's a perfectly innocent explanation."

She shook her head and the tears burst out of her like a pent up flood so I took her in my arms and held her until the sobs started to subside; I led her to a chair by the kitchen table and sat her down. I took the chair next to her and held both of her hands until she had calmed down enough to speak.

"I'm sure there *is* an explanation but I'm not so sure it's innocent."

"What do you mean?"

"Oh Harriet, I think he might be Vernon's accomplice and it's my fault that you and Olive were robbed."

"How on earth can that be?"

"When we were out together he encouraged me to talk about the cafe, who was working when and which were our busiest times. I thought he was just taking an interest in what I did because he really liked me but now I think he might have been pumping me."

Unfortunately I was starting to agree with her; in fact when I'd heard that Vernon was involved I'd started to have my suspicions about Ryan.

"Sophie" I said, "I'm afraid you could be right and I think we should tell the police."

She wiped her sleeve across her eyes and nodded.

"Will you ring them for me Harriet and stay with me when they come.?"

"Of course I will."

D.S. Evans was out of the office when I rang but I left a message asking him to contact me as soon as he was able. He turned up at the cafe shortly after lunch with D.C. Mills in tow. I'd warned Olive and Brad but without going into too much detail, asked them to give Sophie some space. I took the detectives through to the kitchen where Sophie was having her break; we'd be able to talk in private.

Sophie told them all she knew and D.S. Evans said "The reason you've not been able to contact him is because he's in our cells. His real name is Ian Ryan and both he and Paul Vernon are already known to us for a string of similar offences."

"But he told me his name was Ryan Calderbank" said Sophie in disbelief.

"We've known them to use aliases in the past and when we suspected them we showed pictures to your friend, Nina and she identified them.

"And it's all my fault. I gave them the information they needed."

" It might have been that he started seeing you with the intention of getting information" said the D.S., "or he might have made use of the situation when he discovered where you worked."

"Either way I've been played for a mug and brought trouble to my friends."

"You'll not be the first and you'll not be the last," said the detective sergeant, "but if you're willing to testify against him you can help bring him to justice."

"I certainly will," she said.

Something had been bothering me and I had to speak up. "What I don't understand is how some of the stolen goods ended up in Brad's shed."

"Ah" said D.C. Mills, "it turns out that Ryan's mother and Patrick Benfield are brother and sister and we suspect that he paid his uncle a visit hoping he might help him get rid of them, him being in the same trade, so to speak."

D.S. Evans put in "It's even a possibility that he planted the stolen goods there to try and put the blame on Bradley because he seems to have acted when he knew his cousin could be suspected. It seems there has been bad blood between them for some time."

I was too well brought up to say out loud what I was thinking.

"Also", continued the constable "it seems he's used the name Bradley Benfield as an alias before because they're quite alike in looks."

"I'd remarked on that the first time Ryan, I mean Ian, came to pick you up." I said to Sophie. "Did you never notice it?"

"Well now you've pointed it out" she said, "I suppose you're right but it didn't click at the time."

She looked deep in thought. "Harriet, d'you think it could have been Ryan that got that girl pregnant?"

"I wouldn't be surprised."

The detectives stood up to leave. "We'll keep you informed" said D.S. Evans "but I'm afraid we'll have to hang on to the stolen items for a while because they're evidence.

"That's fine," I said, "at least I know I'll get them back eventually."

When they'd gone Sophie stood up straight and said, in a very serious voice, "I'll hand in my notice."

"Whatever for?" I said standing up to face her.

"You can't want me to carry on working here after I betrayed you like that."

"I can and I do," I said, drawing her to me in a hug. "You didn't betray me, you were just naive, thinking everyone is as honest as yourself and I won't condemn you for that."

"But what about Olive?"

"If I know Olive like I think I do, she'll agree with me."

"I've certainly learned a valuable lesson," she said.

I pulled away from her until I held her at arm's length and looked her straight in the eyes.

"Well something good has come out of it then."

I asked Sophie to cover for Olive while she came into the kitchen and let me bring her up to date with events.

"The rotten so and so" she said, when I'd finished. "Using the girl in that way. They should lock him up and throw away the key."

"Not only that, look at the damage he did to Bradley, deliberately setting him up."

"That's besides all the heartbreak and misery their crimes have brought to people."

"Yes" I said, thinking in particular of the Yardley sisters.

I don't know what was said between Sophie and Brad but as the summer passed I watched them become close again, whether or not it would last when they both went off to follow their own educational paths we'd have to wait and see.

My wrist grew stronger and, reluctantly, I made the decision to ring Naiomi to come and pick up Yvette and take her home. She didn't want to go and I was going to miss her but I knew her mum and dad would be missing her more and it was only right that they got to spend some time with her before the summer holidays ended. They might even want to go away together for a break.

"You can come back for a few days at half term" I promised, if it's okay with your mum.

Ian Ryan and Paul Vernon went before the magistrates and were put on remand, bail disallowed for fear of continued offending. As it happened, Sophie didn't need to testify as they both pleaded guilty to all counts in the hope of getting a lighter sentence.

There was only one piece of the jigsaw to be put back into place and that happened unexpectedly on a bright and sunny Wednesday morning at the end of August. It was Brad's day off and I'd left Olive and Sophie running the tearoom while I caught up with some much needed baking. The stock I'd kept in the freezer had dwindled to almost nothing while I'd been out of action.

I'd just taken a lemon meringue pie out of the oven when Olive put her head round the kitchen door. "There's someone here to see you if you've got a minute." she said.

I tutted under my breath but said "Tell them I'll be out as soon as I've put this on the cooling rack."

I put the pie in the rack and hung the oven gloves over a chair back and went into the tearoom. Any annoyance I'd felt at being interrupted melted away like icing sugar on a hot doughnut because sitting at a table by the window were Hilda and Rita Yardley. They were both smiling broadly but it was Rita who said "Can we have some service over here please Mrs. Jones?"

"You certainly can Miss Yardley" I said, taking my pad and pencil from my apron pocket.

The End

Printed in Great Britain
by Amazon

42549925R00050